Three To Ride

Also by Christine Pullein-Thompson in
Dragon Books

Christine Pullein-Thompson

Three To Ride

DRAGON
GRANADA PUBLISHING
London Toronto Sydney New York

Published by Granada Publishing Limited
in Dragon Books 1967
Reprinted 1973, 1975, 1978

ISBN 0 583 30055 3

First published in Great Britain by
Burke Publishing Co Ltd 1958
Copyright © Christine Pullein-Thompson 1958

Granada Publishing Limited
Frogmore, St Albans, Herts AL2 2NF
and
3 Upper James Street, London W1R 4BP
1221 Avenue of the Americas, New York, NY 10020, USA
117 York Street, Sydney, NSW 2000, Australia
100 Skyway Avenue, Toronto, Ontario, Canada M9W 3A6
110 Northpark Centre, 2193 Johannesburg, South Africa
CML Centre, Queen & Wyndham, Auckland 1, New Zealand

Made and printed in Great Britain by
C. Nicholls & Company Ltd
The Philips Park Press, Manchester
Set in Monotype Times

Mrs. Smith packed for David.

"You'd better take all your clothes; it's not as though you've so many," she said.

"Yes, I suppose so," he replied.

Now that the moment had come, he didn't want to leave. He was filled with doubts. He couldn't believe that Major Seely would find him satisfactory, that he could ride well enough to become a working pupil in such a distinguished stable.

He went to the familiar mirror above the old washhandstand with its faded jug and bowl patterned with roses and smoothed his hair. He was on the small side for his sixteen years, and with his dark hair, which fell naturally and persistently over his forehead, and his brown eyes he looked kind, a little bewildered, someone unsure of himself, and perpetually in a dream.

It was his last afternoon at home. Outside the cottage carefully tended flowers bloomed; he could smell them now as he moved to the window, and in every tree there seemed to be a bird singing. May had come with a west wind, and now she warmed the cottage's thatched roof, and the dry soil outside. It was and always had been a wonderful month, thought David, letting his thoughts wander back, trying to remember himself as a little boy first learning to ride at the Riding School across the Common. Afterwards there had been Sinbad, the bad-tempered pony he had been lent by Colonel Lewisham, and the beginning of his friendship with Pat Lewisham. But that was over now; even the Elm Tree Riding School which they had run together was finished. Standing there, he didn't want to remember that part of his life, but a hundred images came rushing to his mind – the first time he had ridden Folly, their success together at the Royal Windsor Show, the wonderful feeling of knowing that she was his own; Pat and himself riding together, hunting together, having tea together in the Hall. Planning the Riding School, their first pupils, buying Tornado at a sale, realising that Pat was tired of their riding school, the beginning of the end. . . .

"I'll have to darn these. You're so hard on your socks, David. And the leathers need sewing on your jodhpurs," his mother said.

They had sold their ponies – all of them except Tornado, Folly, and Pat's Swallow. The selling had been the worst part of all. Colonel Lewisham had insisted that Sinbad and Mistletoe must go; and there seemed no point in keeping little skewbald Suzy. They hadn't sold them very well, and Pat had cried into Mistletoe's mane, which David couldn't understand, because, if she hadn't preferred to be a debutante, nothing need have changed. But then he never had understood Pat.

And now she was going to London and he was going to his first job, and the sign which read The Elm Tree Riding School was in the shed behind the cottage, because David was sentimental and couldn't bear to imagine one of the gardeners at the Hall chopping it for fire-wood.

"We're going to miss you, David; it'll be funny not to hear you clumping down the stairs in the morning. It's like we're getting old," said Mrs. Smith, shutting the suitcase he had bought to take with him.

He turned to his mother, who stood looking at him, her hair pinned behind her ears, wearing a faded pinafore. She had always backed him whenever he had made a decision. She had shared in his joys and sorrows. She had the wisdom of someone who has lived for many years in the country, observing other people, bringing up a family.

"It'll be quieter," David said, searching for words to express what he felt.

"Are you going to say good-bye to *her*?" asked Mrs. Smith with a sniff.

Pat Lewisham had become "her" to Mrs. Smith from the moment she had decided to become a debutante. Mrs. Smith couldn't forgive her for letting down David.

"Might as well. I've got to feed Tornado." He turned away from the window and his mother. Much still remained to be done. There was his tack to be given a last polish, everything to be put ready for the horsebox which would come in the morning to take himself and Tornado from the gentle fields and dreaming rivers of Oxfordshire to Devon, which he knew nothing about, but which he imagined abounded with tea-shops and amenities for tourists.

"It's such a long way," said Mrs. Smith for the twentieth time. "But we'll be thinking of you, your Dad and me. It'll seem funny without you."

"You'll get used to it in time. You'll have less to do; that's one thing. No dirty jodhpurs and dungarees to wash."

"I wonder who'll do your washing," mused Mrs. Smith.

"I'm lodging with one of the grooms," said David, and wondered whether he would have a room to himself. He went down the stairs ahead of his mother, who was talking about his socks again.

"I'd better go and see Tornado now," he said, looking round the cottage, at its shining black range, at the large scrubbed table, and the mantelpiece, where

7

the cups he had won stood, polished by his mother so that you could see your face in them.

"Don't be too late," said Mrs. Smith.

He crossed the Common living old memories. Here he had first learned to vault on to Melody's narrow brown back; here he had hurried in a thunderstorm praying that all his pupils were safe after a runaway. How often he had crossed the Common on his way to the Hall, thousands and thousands of times, and perhaps, except for tomorrow morning this was the last time for many months.

He reached the road, and presently passed the lane and the notice which said *To The Kennels*, which brought back other memories of himself, much younger, working among the hounds as kennel boy. He felt now that he had lived a great many years; yet the days before he started riding remained an insignificant blur. What had he done then? He couldn't even remember. He turned down the stable drive. There were few hoof-prints now on the gravel. Nothing seemed to stir. . . . Once he had seemed to belong here, but now, because Pat had grown tired of their Riding School, he felt quite alien, as he had the first time, when as a small boy he had gone to tea at the Hall.

Only one horse looked over the loose-box doors, and that was Tornado. The Hunt horses were out. Austin, the stud groom, was having an easy time; the other groom was helping on the farm.

He had hoped that Pat would be in the yard waiting for him. But there was no sign of her anywhere, and the saddle-room they had used looked empty with only three saddles and a couple of bridles.

Tornado was lonely and restless. She was sound now after her fall at the One Day Event where David had met Major Seely. David stood looking at her and felt a sense of happiness creep over him; at least he still had

He fetched a rubber and polished her bay coat.

a horse, and Folly was only on loan, so she was still his too. He fetched a rubber and polished her bay coat. She was very fit, though since the One Day Event she had had no oats. She was a difficult horse; she trusted David, but if a stranger rode her she lost her head and became a bucking bronco. .

"We go tomorrow," David told her now. "And you've got to behave, do you hear?"

In reply she nuzzled his pockets.

"It's the beginning of a new era for us," continued David, "Perhaps our big chance."

Outside there were footsteps on the gravel.

"Hullo," said Pat. "I thought you would be here." She had blue eyes, and chestnut hair which glinted copper in the sun; but David hated to look at her now, because she had changed. Once she had had an un-cared-for, windswept look. Now she made him think of people in shiny magazines, people who moved in a different world than his. There was a barrier now between them, which he often felt nothing would break. And because they had spent so much time together he missed the old Pat.

"Are you all packed?" she asked.

"Yes. Mum's packed."

"Excited?"

They were making conversation like strangers.

"Yes and no," he said.

"I'm going to look out for you in *Horse and Hound*. You know: *Promising young David Smith is now riding for* . . ." she said.

"Don't kid yourself," he cried, suddenly wishing that Pat would go, so that he could forget that once there had been horses of their own in the yard, not just Tornado, and pupils, and a telephone in the saddle-room; that once it had been alive, seething with

10

activity, instead of shut up, dead till the hunting season started, as it was now.

"You're miserable, aren't you?" Pat asked.

"No; I'm not," he said, suddenly determined not to care.

"That's all right, then."

He fetched Tornado hay and water. Pat was wearing a flowered cotton dress and high-heeled, sling-back shoes. He supposed that was how she would always dress now – no more dungarees and open-necked shirts.

"Well, I really came to say good-bye – you know, good-bye, good luck and everything. And I brought you this," she said, pressing a small parcel into his hand. He started to open it, but she said, "Not now. Later. Good-bye."

A moment later Pat had disappeared and it seemed another chapter of his life had ended. Inside the package he found a small statuette of a horse in beaten copper.

He stood and looked at it for a long time before he put it in his pocket and started for home.

And now there was twilight on the Common, and he saw two rabbits bobbing among the gorse bushes, the first he had seen since the myxamatosis epidemic. He met several people he knew and they all stopped to talk.

"We hear you're leaving us then, David," they said. And "Well, best of luck in your new job," or simply, "All the best, son."

David had never left home before, and because of this he couldn't imagine himself living anywhere else.

He shook all these people seriously by the hand, saying. "Thank you very much," and "Good-bye."

He found his father was home.

"Well, your last night in the old home. How do you feel, son?" asked Mr. Smith.

"Okay."

"You'll make out all right. Time you left home, though we'll miss you. We'll be thinking of him, won't we, Mother?"

"That's what I keep telling him," said Mrs. Smith.

"I hope Tornado settles down all right. She's so highly strung," said David.

"You and that horse!" cried Mrs. Smith.

It was like any evening at home really, thought David, glancing round the kitchen again, and yet it was his last evening; and in a way he was glad, because now he would be standing on his own feet, learning his own worth; finding whether he had the talent to become a first-class rider, perhaps the best in the land. The future awaited him like a precipice waiting to be climbed, and as his mother passed him a cup of tea he felt capable of climbing it.

"Now, eat a good tea. Remember you've got a long journey in front of you tomorrow and only sandwiches for lunch," said Mrs. Smith.

"Yes, Mum," he said, and saw himself arriving – a stable yard with pigeons fluttering on tiled roofs, Major Seely coming to greet him with outstretched hand.

Arriving

He said good-bye to his mother; she looked suddenly older as she said, "You'll write, won't you? We'll be thinking about you."

"Yes. I'll write," he promised.

He was wearing his best jodhpurs. He had two pairs now, the worst patched all over by his mother. It was early. His parents had risen to say good-bye.

"Remember hard work never hurt anyone, son, but

them what's afraid of it; and it kills them," said his father.

"I will." He was impatient to be gone by this time. He was the last of the Smith children to leave the cottage where they had all grown up. Susan worked now as a secretary in London, and seemed almost a stranger when she came back, smart and efficient, talking about films and nylons. His brothers had both won scholarships to Cambridge and held responsible jobs. He felt like the last fledgeling to leave the nest. He kissed his mother, said, "Good-bye, Dad," and walked away without looking back, carrying his suitcase.

He had packed the horse Pat had given him; simply to remind him of old times, he told himself. Otherwise, he was determined to forget Pat.

A mist hung over the Common, and the same two rabbits were playing among the gorse bushes. He could hear hounds singing as he passed the lane to the kennels, and he thought: That'll fetch Bert (the Huntsman) from his bed.

He had said good-bye to the Hunt staff a couple of days back.

They had wished him all the best, and Bert had said, "We'll miss you, David," like his mother.

He wondered now what it felt like to live in a place where you are new and don't belong. It'll be a new experience, he thought, turning down the drive to the stables.

Tornado whinnied to him. He fetched her a feed – the last of the Riding School's bran and crushed oats.

He stood his tack with his suitcase in the yard. The mist was clearing. Cocks were heralding another day.

Presently he could hear the horse-box. By this time Tornado had finished her feed, so he led her out into the sunlight. He felt quite funny now, looking round the yard; perhaps for the last time, because he would never return unless Pat invited him. He could hear the horse-box coming up the drive and there was a lump in his throat, and he wished that there was someone to say, "Come back soon, David. Don't worry; you'll be a success. There's no doubt about that." But there wasn't; there was just the yard he loved and Tornado turning this way and that in the sunlight. Major Seely had sent the horse-box, and it was large and sumptuous, with a chromium horse on the bonnet.

"Well, David, aren't you going to say good-bye, just for old times' sake?" called a voice, and there was Mr. Austin, half asleep, coming to greet him. And coming towards him from the Hall was Maudie, the Lewisham's help, who had always had a soft spot for David.

"I had to say good-bye," she told him and, leaning forward, kissed his cheek. "Now behave yourself," she added.

Standing there, he felt that these were his real friends.

"Well, if you don't like it, come back. We'll always be able to find you a job in the Hunt stables," said Mr. Austin.

David had never been able to make Mr. Austin understand that, although he loved the hunting field, it was to the show rings and cross-country events that he belonged.

Now he said, "Thank you. I'll never be out of a job, then."

They loaded Tornado. "Okay, then?" asked the driver.

"Best of luck," called Mr. Austin.

"Be good," said Maudie.

The horse-box was moving now. They were leaving; the yard was growing smaller. He was on his way to begin his new life. He stood in the groom's compartment talking to Tornado. He didn't feel strange any more, only determined to succeed.

They turned left when they reached the road. There were people bicycling to work, milk being delivered. The day had really begun. He remembered the days when he had delivered papers, and had belonged to this early-morning world. He had travelled a long way since then, and he meant to travel further. You get what you deserve from life, he thought; one must never blame circumstances for failure; there is always a way round. He had always felt that, though often he was completely devoid of confidence in himself.

He turned to Tornado. "We have great days ahead of us," he said. He leaned out of the window watching familiar fields pass, until they reached country he didn't know – the Vale of Pewsey, vast and open, Swindon – and as they travelled he rode across the landscape, galloping carefree across the Vale, clattering through the busy streets of Swindon.

They stopped at Frome for elevenses.

"We'll be there just about two, mate," said the driver.

"What's the place like?"

"Pretty good."

Tornado was restless, tired of the narrow confines of the horse-box. David was anxious to arrive. Supposing he hated the place? Couldn't get on with the grooms? He was filled with anxiety now.

They drove on through Glastonbury, past small farmsteads, luscious fields, orchards, through stone villages. It looked very different from Oxfordshire to David, and he didn't see many horses, though plenty of prosperous milking cows. What are the people like? he wondered, and found that he was missing Pat. It seemed funny to travel so far with no one to talk to.

They were in Devon when they stopped to eat their sandwiches. It was very hot even for May. The countryside had changed. There were little rolling fields fenced by banks, and most of the villages had one wide street.

"Soon be there now, mate," said the driver.

David fed Tornado, and they fetched her water from a tumbling river nearby. He imagined his mother at home eating by herself in the kitchen, most likely cold meat and pickles and bread and butter, because she never bothered to cook if she was by herself.

What was Pat doing? he wondered. When would she go to London? He supposed she would be visiting Wimbledon, Henley. Would she go to the Royal Windsor Show? he wondered.

"Better get going now, mate," said the driver.

The climbed back into the horse-box.

"Wouldn't you rather ride in the cab?" asked the driver.

"No, thanks. I think I'd better stay with the mare." Tornado was very restless now; she chewed the partition, and several times set into the back of the compartment with her heels. And David wanted to keep his eyes glued to the window, because any place might be Major Seely's Hampton House. A great many old fears came back to him now; he started to doubt his riding ability; to wonder why he had ever accepted the job. He felt he would have done better to become nothing more than a groom, under a good stud groom.

Then they were turning down a drive and he could see a clock tower, rows of loose boxes, horses looking across a sunlit yard. He felt quite sick then. Everything seemed bigger than he had expected, smarter. He could see the chimneys of the house, an elegant garden. I'm here, he thought. I'm making a new beginning. This is my testing-ground. Here I shall know whether I will ever become a first-class rider or whether I belong for ever to the ranks of mediocrity.

The horse-box stopped.

"Here we are, mate," called the driver.

All around were horses looking at them with inquisitive eyes. As David stepped out on to the gravelled yard, a groom emerged from a loose-box.

"Hullo. So you're David," he said. "How's the mare? Did she travel all right?"

"Not too badly."

The driver was letting down the ramp. The fair girl David had seen at the One Day Event appeared.

"Hullo. You've arrived, then," she said.

Tornado came out of the box with a rush. Her tail bandage had slipped; she had rubbed one of her hocks against the back of the partition.

"Useful sort of mare," said the groom.

"She's lovely, isn't she?" asked the girl. They put Tornado in a box which stood ready.

The driver said, "All the best, mate," and got into his cab and drove away, leaving David's suitcase standing small and forlorn in the yard.

"Have you had some dinner?" asked the groom.

David had time to look at his companions now. The girl was slim, with a great deal of fair soft hair. She was taller than David and, he guessed, about his own age. The groom wore breeches and gaiters, braces, a flannel shirt without a collar, and working boots.

"Well, you'd better come along and see the Missis. You're lodging with us," he said.

There was no sign of Major Seely; and now David could hardly remember what he looked like.

"I'm Bates, Jimmy Bates," said the groom. "The girl you were talking to is Sheila; then there's the stud

17

groom, Mr. Booth. He runs the place when the governor's away."

"Is he away now?" asked David.

"No. But he'll be going away later on."

They had been walking behind the stables. Now they came to a small, single-storied building.

"My place," said Mr. Bates. "Olive, 'ere's our lodger come to see you."

Olive was younger than Mr. Bates, David thought, with dark hair which was still in curlers.

"Pleased to meet you I'm sure," she said, shaking his hand.

His room was small, with lino on the floor, a modern bed, a small mat, and an armchair.

"I hope you'll be comfortable here. Would you like a cup of tea? Have you had dinner?"

They all had a cup of tea in the kitchen. Then David and Mr. Bates returned to the stables.

"Have a look round the horses. I must be getting on. The governor should be here any time," he said.

The horses were large, well built, except for one dun mare who was little more than fifteen hands. There was a chestnut-stallion, who stood in a box apart from the others. There was a hunter mare with a foal which David judged to be little more than a week old.

He couldn't help wondering which horse he would ride. Or would he try all the rideable ones?

"Feel strange?" asked Sheila. "The stallion's called Royal Majesty – Majesty for short. Don't you think he's lovely?" Her hands were full of grooming kit. "Here comes old Booth," she cried suddenly and fled.

David didn't like Mr. Booth; some instinct in his being warned him against him, though why exactly he couldn't have said. He didn't like his small grey eyes, which didn't look at you. Nor the way he said, "So you're David Smith."

18

"You look as though you need a job. There's a pile of dirty tack in the saddle-room. What about getting down to it?" asked Mr. Booth.

"Yes. Right you are." David found the tack.

"There's a hot tap outside on the right," called Sheila from across the yard.

There were seven dirty saddles and nine dirty bridles. He started to work. Outside Mr. Booth was feeding cut grass to the horses. Jimmy Bates was taking a skip round the boxes. Sheila appeared to be dressing a black horse's off fore.

Tornado was walking round and round her box. The clock in the tower said two forty-five.

Presently a Scottie, a poodle, and spaniel came across the yard, followed by Major Seely. He spoke to Mr. Booth, looked across to the saddle-room. David had forgotten how nimble he appeared, and he looked every inch a horseman.

"Hullo, David. So you've arrived. Had a good journey?" he said, coming across the yard.

They looked at Tornado together. "Nice little mare; but she needs to be a bit fitter," he said. "Has Jimmy showed you where you're lodging? Is it all right? Do you think you'll be comfortable?"

"Yes, thank you, sir."

They stood for some time in silence, leaning over the loose-box door looking at Tornado.

"Well, we'll have a little school this evening – see how you ride," said Major Seely. "The horses will go better when it's a bit cooler."

He walked round the rest of the horses with Mr. Booth. David returned to the dirty tack, and Sheila appeared and said, "This is really my job."

They worked in silence for a time until Sheila said, "I wouldn't be in your shoes."

19

"Why? I like the look of everything," David answered.

"Major Seely yells like anything. He'll have you bumping round the paddock without stirrups. He'll lunge you for hours. I'd rather be just a groom, thank you."

"I don't care so long as it improves my riding."

"If you're a fanatic, that's all right. I like other things – dancing, the cinema. I've heard Major Seely say to people, 'If you've enough energy left after two hours in the school with me to want to dance, it simply means you haven't been working enough.' I have really."

David felt his heart sinking. He longed suddenly now for the freedom of the Elm Tree Riding School, for the days when he and Pat had stood in the middle of a school instructing pupils. In spite of being poor, he had always been more or less his own master. Now he was a working pupil with pocket money of a pound a week and lodgings paid for by Major Seely.

He realised now that he had never valued his freedom enough. He thought, I can always leave, but at the same time condemned the thought, because how could he return home and admit failure? He imagined his parents' faces, though soon enough they would be on his side, his mother condemning Major Seely as she now condemned Pat.

He thought: I shall have to stick it out for a bit, for a month at least.

"That's finished. Are you going to help me fill up the water-buckets?" asked Sheila, hanging up the last bridle.

He rode two horses that evening, big, honest, bay Jolly Roger and the dun mare, Sandstorm. As he rode the bay, he imagined his father calling, "You look like a tomtit on a round of beef, son," a favourite saying of his; and the bay did feel large, his ears seemed miles away, and David's heels only reached halfway down his enormous sides. The first time he jumped he fell off, banging his nose and jarring his back, but remembering to spring to his feet and run after the bay calling, "Sorry, sir."

Major Seely stayed where he was leaning against his shooting stick watching David. Jolly Roger halted and stood snorting. He'll never want me to stay on here now, thought David. Why did I ever come? I knew I wasn't good enough. He caught the bay and struggled back into the saddle with an effort.

"He feels big, doesn't he? You're not used to big horses?" asked Major Seely.

"No. I'm not really." He hated to admit it.

He jumped the bay again, staying on, but only just, and feeling more depressed each moment.

"That's better. Now we'll try Sandstorm," said Major Seely.

She was an easier ride and very clever. He enjoyed jumping her.

"She suits you better. Tomorrow we'll do some work on the flat," said Major Seely.

They put Sandstorm away, and stood talking for a time about Oxfordshire, about shows, about Sandstorm's possibilities.

"I'd like to see you on your own mare tomorrow," said Major Seely.

They walked round the horses saying little. Tornado whinnied to David.

It was still a lovely day, warm and tranquil, more like early September than May.

"I'm keeping you from your supper. Leave the tack till the morning."

David had had tea with Jimmy Bates and Olive. There had been pilchards in tomato sauce as well as bread and butter, strong tea and little fancy cakes. He had complimented Olive on the cakes, though he preferred his mother's. Now he said, "Well, good night, sir."

He felt rather lonely as he wandered in the direction of the Bates's bungalow. It made him think of walking home across the Common after a happy day at the Riding School, imagine his mother in a faded overall pouring him tea, his father coming in. He felt nostalgic suddenly for familiar things, and was certain at the same time that nothing would ever be the same again. When he returned home he would see everything through new eyes because he had been away. How would the cottage look then? he wondered. He imagined everything would look smaller – his bedroom, the kitchen, the cottage itself.

"Well, how did it go?" asked Jimmy as he entered the bungalow.

"Did you fall off?"

The Bates were consoling.

"That's always the way," said Jimmy.

"Never mind. Major Seely will understand. Won't he, Jimmy? I expect you were nervous," said Olive.

There was bread and cheese, pickles, a little cold meat, tea again.

22

"Make yourself at home," said Olive.

He realised now how tired he was; it seemed to come over him like a wave. Years might have passed since early morning.

"The governor's a good sort," said Jimmy.

"Would you like a bath? We have a bath," said Olive with pride.

He had always bathed at home in a tin bath in front of the range.

"I lit the copper specially," said Olive.

They sat for a time after supper. Then David found his way to the bath, which was in the wash-house, and baled water from the copper. He felt too tired now to imagine anything. He only wanted to be in bed, to sleep and sleep.

Jimmy and Olive called, "Good night" through the door. "Don't stop there too long. We'll call you in the morning."

He switched off the lights on the way to his room. It was dark outside now. One of the horses was neighing and he wondered whether it could be Tornado.

He clambered into his bed, which was modern with a walnut headpiece, and switched off the light. What a fool I was to fall off. I wish Major Seely had said something, he thought. He felt now that he would like to take a look at Tornado. Did she feel strange? he wondered, but before he could summon strength to get out of bed, cross the yard in the dark and find her box, he fell asleep.

The next day he rode a little better. He spent a long time bumping round the school without stirrups, just as Sheila had prophesied. As he schooled Tornado, instructed by Major Seely, he could feel her going better each moment, and Major Seely was encouraging.

"That's good. That's very good," he said, and, "You're sitting better now. Drive, more drive, drive."

In the afternoon he was told to hack Jolly Roger, and Sheila was told to escort him on Parisian, an excitable thoroughbred. He felt much happier now. He was certain that his riding had already started to improve. Immense opportunities seemed to lie ahead. For the first time he could remember running the Riding School with Pat without pain.

"Well, do you like it here?" asked Sheila as they turned out of the yard, beneath a dappled sky.

"Yes; and I'm learning a lot," he said.

"Gosh, you are keen, aren't you?"

"I suppose so. I've always been keen on riding ever since I was a little boy."

"I'm too lazy. Besides, I'm going to get married next year," she said.

"Congratulations," exclaimed David, remembering his brother Michael's wedding, himself throwing confetti, the reception afterwards in the Village Hall, how strange his parents were in their best clothes.

"I haven't a ring or anything yet. It's just an understanding, if you know what I mean," said Sheila.

It wasn't like riding with Pat. Sheila talked without a pause; but the countryside was beautiful, and in the distance they could see the moors. And Jolly Roger was a calm, pleasant hack, well-schooled and well-mannered.

"Leonard was in the same lodgings as me; now he's at an agricultural college. When he's got his diploma, we're going to get married."

"And have a farm?" asked David.

There were banks on each side of them festooned with

24

flowers. How do you jump a bank? he wondered. Do people jump them hunting? What happens when a horse hits a bank?

He turned to ask Sheila, but she was still talking about Leonard.

"He's taller than you are," she said, "And he has lovely dark, curly hair."

David didn't know what reply was expected, so he said nothing. The fields on each side of them now were filled with ewes and lambs. The clouds had gone and it was another warm day. David rolled up his sleeves.

"Let's trot," suggested Sheila, pushing Parisian with her heels.

They trotted along a dusty lane, forded a river, walked up a slope strewn with boulders, trotted again, and all the time Sheila was talking. The horses were sweating now and David started to slow down Jolly Roger, but Sheila continued trotting, shouting remarks back over her shoulder.

"Booth's an old so-and-so. Jimmy's not so bad. The governor's fair, I'll say that for him, but he thinks too much of Booth," she called.

By Parisian's behaviour, David guessed that they had turned for home. Sheila was sitting anyhow and Parisian was breaking into a canter at intervals and throwing his head in all directions. Sheila continued talking.

"He used to jump a lot – jumped for England, someone said. You should see his lounge; it's full of photos. What would you say his age was?"

And then it happened; one moment Parisian was tearing along in front, with Sheila bobbing about on top, her pale hair windswept like a galloping palomino's mane, the next they seemed to be pitching forward, folding up in front of his eyes. David wanted to cry, "Hi, stop! Hold him together. Collect him . . . drive,

25

drive, drive. . . ." But it was too late now. Sheila had let Parisian tear along, unbalanced, throwing his head about, off the bit, all over the place, and now he was falling and there was nothing David could do but watch. Parisian fell on his knees. Sheila went on over his shoulder. For a moment time seemed to stand still. Then the dark brown thoroughbred scrambled to his feet, stepped on the end of his reins, threw his head in the air, trotted away, leaving a trail of blood behind him. His knees are broken, David thought; he's scarred for ever and ever. Why didn't I say "Let's walk" to Sheila? I knew she was riding badly. Why didn't I do something?

He looked at Sheila now, who lay in a heap, groaning faintly. He wanted to catch Parisian first. But supposing Sheila was badly hurt? He couldn't simply leave her there and follow Parisian.

He dismounted, bent over Sheila.

"Are you hurt? Can you move?" he asked.

"I don't know. I feel awful," she cried. "What will Major Seely say?"

He didn't know. He didn't like to think. He wished that Sheila would get up. He couldn't see Parisian now.

"Try to get up," he said.

She stood up. She wasn't hurt; he could see that now. He was seized by a wave of anger.

"You aren't hurt at all. You were simply pretending," he cried, starting to follow the trail of blood, imagining joint oil leaking from gashed knees, trying to imagine how he would feel if someone had let Tornado stumble through bad riding and ruined her for ever.

He could hear Sheila calling something to him from behind, but he didn't listen. He had eyes now for only the trail of blood. He reached a road and saw Parisian

26

Parisian fell on his knees. Sheila went on over his shoulder.

grazing on a bank fifty yards ahead. Approaching him, he noticed how well he was put together. He had tremendous depth of girth, a long, sloping shoulder, beautiful limbs. He couldn't find fault with his conformation, and it dawned on David that Parisian was probably a show horse, and that made everything ten times worse, because what use would he be for a show horse with scarred knees? Always he would be marked down – his career was ruined.

Parisian raised his head and watched David approach. "Whoa, little horse, whoa," said David.

Already there were flies buzzing round Parisian's knees. David wanted to run, to drive them off. He couldn't bear the thought of them sucking Parisian's blood, perhaps infecting his wounds. But he restrained himself, because if he ran Parisian might trot away, and that would be disastrous.

Another moment and he had hold of the broken rein, was bending down looking at two bleeding knees, while Jolly Roger stood patiently watching. One was worse than the other; one was very bad indeed. David felt quite sick as he looked at the worst. It was deep and full of grit and dirt, and bled slowly and obstinately, but not fast enough to warrant a torniquet, he judged.

"It wasn't my fault," cried Sheila, suddenly behind him. "I couldn't help him falling, silly horse."

She was near to tears.

"How far are we from home?" asked David, suddenly calm.

"About a mile."

"We'd better have a box, then. Can you take Jolly Roger and get someone to come with a trailer or something?"

"Is he very bad? What will Major Seely say? It wasn't my fault."

"I'll stay with Parisian," said David. "Accidents will happen," he added, recalling a saying of his mother's.

Sheila mounted Jolly Roger.

"Go carefully. Don't hurry," said David, wondering whether she had ever ridden the bay before.

He talked to Parisian while he waited. "You'll be all right soon," he said, "We'll get you home, and then you can have some lovely hay and cut grass. You'll be all right soon."

But he thought at the same time: Will he? What will they do with him if he's stiff in front for ever?

Time seemed to pass very slowly. More and more flies gathered until they were swarming round Parisian as though they had their own form of telepathy and could send messages to one another, "Injured horse on bank. Very tasty."

I should have told Sheila to telephone for the vet, too, David thought. Perhaps Major Seely isn't at home. Perhaps Mr. Booth gives anti-tetanus injections himself; some stud grooms do.

At last he saw a car and trailer coming. He started to wave, and saw that Mr. Booth was driving, with Sheila sitting beside him.

"Here's the trailer. You'll be home soon now," he told Parisian.

"Now what's 'appened?" asked Mr. Booth, getting out of the car and bending down to look at Parisian's knees.

"Done them good and proper, hasn't he? Clumsy beggar. We'd better get him home and have a proper look at them."

Parisian was very stiff now. He would only move his forelegs with a great deal of persuasion. They had to push and coax him into the trailer.

"He'll never make a show horse now," said Mr.

29

Booth gloomily, starting up the engine. "What were you two doing anyway? Racing, I suppose."

"We were trotting," said David.

"He just fell. I don't know why," added Sheila.

"One can't trust anyone nowadays. All they want to do is tear about," replied Mr. Booth.

David didn't say anything. He sensed that Mr. Booth didn't like him, and the thought filled him with gloom.

And he felt gloomy, too, because he had known Sheila was riding Parisian badly and had done nothing.

But nothing would silence Sheila's tongue.

"He was very fresh. He wanted to be in front all the time, didn't he, David? It excites him being in company. It wasn't my fault," she said.

That's what small children say. They break things, fall down, forget to shut gates, and they always say, "It wasn't my fault," thought David.

"I don't like to think what the governor will say," said Mr. Booth, turning up the drive.

Sheila was crying now. "I wish Leonard was here," she whispered to David. "It wasn't my fault, was it?"

"No; it wasn't. It might happen to anyone," said David. Jimmy Bates was taking a skip round the boxes. Tornado was munching a feed. The sun had turned a fiery red in the sky.

"I'm sorry for you two. What were you up to?" called Jimmy.

"They were only trotting," said Mr. Booth with sarcasm.

"*He*'ll be back presently," said Jimmy, crossing the yard to look at Parisian.

"Proper mucked himself up, hasn't he?" asked Mr. Booth.

"Doesn't look too good," agreed Jimmy. "Never

mind, Sheila. Cheer up. It happens to the best of us. When I was a lad I lost a racehorse. Went right through Newmarket it did, the blighter. . . ."

"Come on. Let's get him in a box," interrupted Mr. Booth. They half carried Parisian out of the trailer, put him in a box, looked at his knees again.

"I'd better give him a shot," said Mr. Booth.

Sheila made herself scarce. "You get on and clean the tack. You've done enough damage for the day," Mr. Booth told David.

He spoke to Tornado, found Sheila in the saddle-room.

"What do you think Major Seely will say? It's all right for you. No one can blame you," said Sheila.

"Mr. Booth seems to think it's all my fault," said David.

"Don't listen to him," advised Sheila.

They cleaned tack and Sheila continued talking, but David didn't bother to listen any more. He saw himself being lectured by Major Seely, disbelieved by Mr. Booth, and life seemed very hard indeed.

Schooling

But David didn't see Major Seely that evening, for when he and Sheila had finished the tack, Mr. Booth said, "Now you two had better scram. I'll deal with the fireworks."

He left the yard regretfully. He hated the thought of Mr. Booth telling his version of the accident; and he didn't want to go to bed with a cloud still hanging over him.

The Bates had gone out, leaving tea waiting on the table. He ate a little bread and butter, roamed round

31

the room, wondered whether Major Seely had returned yet.

After a time he wandered outside, down a lane, across two fields, past a little cottage and a woman fetching water from a spring. He felt homesick now. He wanted to talk to someone about the accident, to ask them whether it was partly his fault; he remembered the saying, *A trouble shared is a trouble halved*, and wondered whether it was true.

When he went to bed he slept badly, and dreamed he was in Oxfordshire again arguing with Pat about Tornado.

He wakened with a start when Jimmy Bates, knocking on the door, said, "Six-thirty." He couldn't believe the night had passed so quickly. For a moment he thought, Where am I? before he remembered.

When he reached the kitchen Jimmy had already made the early-morning tea, and passed David a cup and a biscuit.

"You look glum enough. What's eating you?" asked Jimmy.

"Nothing really," David said.

It was a cloudy morning, but very warm. David found a fork and started to muck-out Tornado. Presently Sheila looked over the door.

"Was there a rumpus last night?" she asked.

"I don't know."

"Have you spoken to Mr. Booth?"

"Not yet."

Parisian's knees were swathed in bandages. He looked very sorry for himself.

When the mucking-out was done, David returned to the bungalow with Jimmy for breakfast. Olive was up by this time and their bacon and eggs was ready.

"How's the horse?" she asked.

"Pretty bad," replied Jimmy.

"Poor thing."

"David seems to think it was his fault. Don't ask me why. He wasn't on top," Jimmy said.

There was a letter for David from his mother. She wondered whether he had arrived safely, because he hadn't written. He remembered now that he had promised to send a postcard on arrival.

"What you need is a bike; get out a bit," Jimmy said.

There wasn't any news in his mother's letter. "Everything is the same," she wrote. "But your room looks empty. We haven't changed anything."

"Come on. Back to the stables," said Jimmy.

David continued to dread meeting Major Seely, but when he did neither of them mentioned Parisian.

"I'd like you to ride Tornado first. Give her a bit of a school. I've got to go to the office now, but when I get back we'll have out Sandstorm. There's a show next Saturday I'd like her to go to."

He called his dogs and went away. "What did he say?" asked Sheila, appearing as though by magic.

"Nothing. Didn't mention it."

"Old Booth says he carried on something awful last night," Sheila said.

"I think Mr. Booth has a grudge against us," replied David.

"He has against you with reason, I suppose. Didn't you know his son used to jump for Major Seely?" asked Sheila.

"No. No one told me."

"He pinched some money or something. He's in Borstal or somewhere. Jimmy told me," Sheila said.

"That explains a lot," David said, and in a sense the news was a relief to him, because at least he knew now why Mr. Booth disliked him.

He schooled Tornado for an hour; then after putting

33

her away he put some tack on Sandstorm and waited for Major Seely. The vet. had been to see Parisian and had pulled a long face.

"I can't say what sort of recovery he'll make. He certainly won't be fit to show after this," he had said.

Sheila was gloomy, Mr. Booth in a bad temper.

"I should take the mare out, loosen her up a bit before the governor comes," Jimmy advised David.

Sandstorm was very fresh. Someone had put up the jumps. Sheila was raking the tan in the school, which was outside and fenced by high split oak, so that the occupants couldn't be distracted.

Presently Major Seely arrived and David, thinking, Take the bull by the horns, said, "I'm sorry about our disastrous ride yesterday."

He noticed now that Major Seely looked very tired and thought, I've probably chosen the wrong moment, but Major Seely only said, "Don't worry, David. Things like that just happen. It's a shame, but there it is."

"I'm sorry all the same," said David.

"I think we all are," replied Major Seely.

When David jumped Sandstorm she performed very well, jumping the put-up course clear, while David sat still, letting her judge her own distance, only once collecting her a little when he felt her losing the rhythm of her stride.

"That's very good indeed. We'll enter her on Saturday. Well done. Now will you fetch your mare and see how she does round the course," said Major Seely.

He put Sandstorm away. He felt much better now. Jumping Sandstorm had brought back his confidence in himself. He felt capable of anything now.

34

Tornado jumped well, only knocking the oxer with her hind legs. David couldn't remember a time when she had done better.

"Excellent," called Major Seely. "Just jump the oxer again. Do you want to take her on Saturday too?"

"Yes, please, sir," called David.

The next few days were happy ones: the sun shone, Parisian's knees began to heal. David's riding improved; he started to settle down. He met Mrs. Seely for the first time; she was tall and friendly, and she suggested that he should come to the house for tea when he had time to spare. He had saved his first pound and tried to decide whether to buy a dog or a bicycle when he had saved some more. The approaching show loomed high on the horizon, but Major Seely had said, "Don't worry about it, David. It's just a try-out. We're not expecting brilliance this year. Next season will be a different matter." And so he wasn't worried, but determined to take it in his stride like a daily event. He had written to his mother – a long, descriptive letter; so now his conscience was clear in that respect. And he was beginning to like Devon, to feel at home among the banks, to like the narrow roads, the shallow, rushing rivers, the quiet villages.

Sheila still talked incessantly when they were together, but he had discovered that she didn't expect an answer and wasn't offended if he appeared to ignore her.

Sometimes he missed the easy comradeship which he had enjoyed with Pat in the old days, but as time passed he missed her less, and there was always Jimmy to talk to in the evenings.

Tornado and Sandstorm continued to go well, and he felt more at home on Jolly Roger now, who was destined for One and Three Day Events the following year.

"I think he should do well. He's bold with plenty of endurance, and by then his dressage should be better," Major Seely said.

On the Friday before the show Sheila helped him clean his tack. She was to go with him and Major Seely in the trailer.

"Aren't you nervous? I should be. It must be awful jumping someone else's horses," she said.

"One has to keep a sense of proportion," David answered. "One can't do better than one can."

He still wasn't nervous; he had eaten a good tea. He felt happier, happier than he had for months. Everything seemed to add up to what he wanted – to become a great rider, to ride for England. He could see himself forging ahead, improving every day, until next year he was riding Jolly Roger in all the biggest events – Badminton, Stowell Park, perhaps even abroad.

And his own horse Tornado should be in the first rank by then, and there was still Sandstorm. He felt like singing at the top of his voice as he cleaned his jumping saddle. I have three to ride, he thought. Three first-class horses.

"This is going to be a wonderful summer," he told Sheila.

"Why on earth?"

"I don't know," he replied. "It just is."

"You're a funny one – one moment gloomy, the next moment full of the joy of living. Now, Leonard . . ." began Sheila.

He didn't listen because he had heard all about Leonard already. He let his thoughts drift back home, to the day he returned for a visit, perhaps with his dog if he had one.

Once a month he had a whole week-end off. He would go home then, he decided, and saw the cottage, the familiar kitchen, his parents. He couldn't help wondering about Pat. Where was she now? When would he see her again? Would he bump into her at one of the shows?

"It's all done. Wake up, dreamer," exclaimed Sheila.

He looked at Sandstorm and Tornado before he walked to the bungalow. Their tails had been recently pulled, their coats shone. Tornado looked completely different to the vicious mare he and Pat had bought at a horse-sale roughly nine months ago. Then she had looked sad; there had been deep poverty marks in her quarters; she had been almost unrideable. Now she appeared well fed, her eye was kind, her quarters round. She looked worth three figures, and she's mine, David reminded himself with a feeling of pride.

"All ready for tomorrow?" asked Olive as he entered the bungalow.

"Yes. All set."

He went to bed early; it was a cloudy night, with rain in the air, which had made Olive say at supper, "I hope it keeps fine for you. I wish we were going along too. Don't you, Jimmy?"

"It's only a little show. We'll wait till 'e's at the White City or Harringay. That'll be worth seeing," Jimmy had said.

David thought about that when he was in bed – Harringay and the White City, jumping in a lighted arena. It was something which had belonged to dreams before; now it was within the realms of possibility. Everything seemed a little too good to be true. Wouldn't Mum be pleased? he thought, and imagined her talking to him before he went into the arena at Harringay, the familiar shopping-bag in her hand.

He had always placed the big shows far away in the future, but now his companions talked about them like any ordinary event.

"We must try to qualify Tornado and Sandstorm for the Foxhunter Event at Harringay in October," Major Seely had said.

"I hope I go with you when you take the horses to the White City," said Sheila.

As though it was all already settled. Only Mr. Booth remained sceptical, and now David knew about his son he didn't bother about Mr. Booth any more.

He fell asleep quite soon on the night before the show, and didn't hear the storm which broke in the small hours, the rain which lashed his window, the crashes of thunder; nor did the jagged flashes of lightning waken him.

In the morning when he got up, still optimistic, the sky was clear, a breeze stirred the gravel in the yard – everything seemed to point to a fine day.

Well Done!

"Still cocksure?" asked Sheila when he appeared in the stable yard wearing a thick, faded jersey knitted by his mother.

"Not cocksure. I don't expect to win. I'm treating today as a kind of trial, as a testing-ground," David answered. He had learned by experience to expect little rather than much. He found that way he wasn't continually disappointed; more often he had a pleasant surprise.

Mr. Booth had already fed the horses. He was

38

usually in the yard first. It was a matter of pride with him; he liked to feel that he was better than his inferiors.

"I'll see to Sandstorm. You get on with your own mare," he told David.

Nothing reminded David of preparing for a show at Elm Tree Riding School; there he and Pat had risen in the small hours; pupils had arrived on bicycles and were difficult to recognise in dawn's murky light. There had been something unusual, almost festive, about the washing and the plaiting, the hurry and the flurry. There had been breakfast eaten hastily in the Lewishams' kitchen; the mounting excitement as the time for starting drew near.

But today the horses weren't even to be plaited. Their daily grooming was always lengthy, so there was little extra polishing to be done. Mr. Booth checked the belongings to be taken.

"Don't forget to put the screws in their shoes if it's wet," he told Sheila. "There are the feeds all weighed out."

Once David had groomed Tornado, there was little left for him to do, so he wandered back to the bungalow and gave his clothes an extra brush over while Olive prepared breakfast.

"I've cut you some sandwiches. Do you want something to drink, or will you get something from the refreshment tent?" she asked.

He was ready far too early. After breakfast he stood about the yard feeling conspicuous in his best riding clothes. The sky was quite clear; it was difficult to believe that there had been a storm in the night.

Tornado was restless, as though she knew something unusual was to happen. Jimmy said, "Well, best of luck. I must lunge the stallion now or the governor will create. Don't fall off. Anything but that."

At last Major Seely appeared, and backed the car out of the garage, and with Mr. Booth's help connected the trailer. Sandstorm loaded without trouble; but Tornado was suspicious and ill at ease, until finally David rode her up the ramp, jumping off as she entered the trailer.

Mrs. Seely appeared, and David and Sheila climbed into the back of the car.

"How do you feel, David – nervous?" asked Mrs. Seely. She was dressed in a checked suit, and carried a picnic set. With her came the dogs, wagging their tails madly at the thought of an outing.

"Not very," David admitted.

"Perhaps you're one of those lucky people who don't get nervous," said Mrs. Seely.

The horses travelled well. Sheila and David remained almost entirely silent during the whole journey. David could only imagine that Sheila was overcome by shyness in the presence of her employer. He was feeling shy himself, but it was an old feeling: he had always been intimidated by people socially better off than himself, though after a time he had felt quite at home with Pat's father, who owned the Hall, and was a retired Colonel and a Master of Foxhounds into the bargain. But for a long time he had found it difficult to get on with the better-off children at the Pony Club; only after he had won the Juvenile Jumping at the Royal Windsor Show had he felt on equal terms with them. He had always found it necessary to prove his own worth to himself. Pat had maintained that he suffered from an inferiority complex. But he didn't think that was true; he was simply a cat which walked alone, as one of his brothers had told him; and because he had one ambition which meant almost more to him than anything else on earth, he hadn't much time for other people.

"A penny for your thoughts?" whispered Sheila as they reached the show-ground.

"Not worth the penny. I bet I know what yours were, though," David replied.

"What?"

"You were thinking about Leonard."

"How did you guess?"

"Because you nearly always are," David replied.

The ground was bright with tents. Hunters were being judged in the ring. Horses were everywhere.

Major Seely parked the car under a clump of trees.

"Time for a look-round before we unbox," he said, springing lightly from the car, looking less tired today, so that David thought: He's one of those ageless people, who drop dead quite suddenly and, to everyone's surprise, are found to be eighty or ninety.

"Come on. Let's hurry," said Sheila. David looked at the horses before he followed Sheila and Major and Mrs. Seely across the show-ground.

He felt very much at home now; he loved the bustle, the thudding of hoofs on turf, the gleaming tack on the horses being ridden, the air of excitement and suspense. It seemed to lift his spirits, until he was filled with elation. Crossing the show-ground, he could only think, as he had on other occasions: This is my life. Here I belong. Success or failure, I shall never desert this world of horses and horsemen.

He wanted to stand and take it all in; to lean against the ring ropes and dream about his future.

"A good class for hunters; not often you see so many in the ring at once at this sort of show," said Major Seely. "What do you think of them, David?"

He didn't consider himself a good judge of a horse. His heart was in show jumping, cross-country events, hunter trials, "Pretty good lot," he replied.

"Not quite top class. But a nice little lot, all the same," agreed Major Seely.

David kept forgetting that he was so far from home and expected to bump into friends – Pony Club officials, Merry, Richard, people he had met in the hunting field.

They all stopped, leaned against the ring ropes, looked at the hunters. Several times Major Seely met people he knew. Once he introduced David.

"This is my new rider. He's jumping today," he said.

The Grade C Jumping was at twelve o'clock. Presently Mrs. Seely wandered to the Secretary's tent, taking the dogs with her, to collect David's number, while Major Seely, David, and Sheila went back to the trailer and unboxed Tornado, whom David had decided to ride first.

"I want you to ride her round for a bit before you take a look at the course. Sheila will walk Sandstorm around until you want her. You're fifth in the ring on Tornado, according to the programme," said Major Seely.

David still felt quite calm – uncannily calm, he told himself as he bridled Tornado. The hunters had left the ring, and had been replaced by ponies and children on leading reins.

More people were arriving all the time. David mounted Tornado, who felt fresh and ill at ease; her back was up, her neck like a ramrod, for a few moments all her schooling seemed forgotten. Then she relaxed, dropped her nose, went into her bridle like a dressage horse, which made David realise how much she had improved since coming to Devon.

Soon the jumps were being arranged in the ring –

42

gaily-painted red and white bars, two gates, a wall, dark brush fences. The crowd was becoming thicker along the ring ropes, spectators were climbing on the roofs of cars, practice jumps were appearing. The elegant hunters had gone; instead, a great variety of horses was emerging from trailers, horse-boxes, and from the road – cobs, thoroughbreds with goose rumps, thickset jumpers, all sorts, all shapes. Riders in black coats were fewer; there were more martingales and odd contraptions to be seen.

Presently Major Seely took Tornado.

"Have a look at the jumps while you can," he said.

It was a relatively simple course: the two brush fences had guard rails, the stile was on the flimsy side, but the combination of two gates was straightforward, and there wasn't a twist or a sharp corner to unbalance Tornado.

"Not too difficult, is it?" asked Major Seely as David mounted again.

"No, sir. The stile looks the worst fence to me," David replied.

He still felt calm as he stood in the collecting ring waiting for his number to be called.

Everyone else there seemed to know each other, which gave him the feeling of an outsider. Tornado had been entered under his own name, so that there was nothing to tell anyone that he was Major Seely's new working pupil. Walking Tornado backwards and forwards across the collecting ring, he longed suddenly for Pat to be beside him; he couldn't remember a show without her; she had always been there, "nannying" him, as she called it. But that's past, he decided, and the past should be nothing more than a signpost to the future. He turned his attention to the ring and refused to see the image which obscured the jumps of a girl

43

with chestnut hair who said, "You'll be a great rider one day, David. I know you will."

A few more minutes and the collecting ring steward was saying, "You next. Are you ready?" And he was collecting Tornado, riding into the ring, not seeing the crowd, but only the jumps, thinking. Nothing else matters. Steady, Tornado. Steady – turning towards the first brush fence, remembering the guard rails on each side, letting his mare judge her own distance. It's like poetry, he thought, approaching the stile; like beautiful music. There must be no rough edges, no wrenching. One's performance must be as smooth as running water. Tornado tipped the stile, but it didn't fall; she cleared the gates with ease, jumped the wall with care, lengthened her stride for the triple. The crowd was quite silent; leaning against the ring ropes, Major and Mrs. Seely watched. There was a slight turn before the second brush fence; Tornado changed legs, cleared the brush, increased her speed for the hog's-back. Nearly home, thought David, collecting his mare for the upright fence, feeling a rush of joy as they approached the last fence of all, a Sussex gate.

"He's certainly got something," said Mrs. Seely.

"He's a lot better than Tony Booth," said her husband. I've done a clear round, thought David. Oh, Tornado, you're wonderful, and I never thought you would make a show jumper.

"Jolly good," called Sheila, running to meet him. "Here. Take your second horse."

He found some oats in his pocket for Tornado before he mounted Sandstorm. The groans from the crowd told him that a popular competitor had knocked a fence. For the first time he noticed that the day was unbearably hot.

"Well done, David. A very nice round indeed," commented Major Seely.

44

"Thank you, sir."

"Best of luck," muttered Sheila.

He was anxious now; he wanted to do as well on Major Seely's horse as he had on his own. But another clear round seemed like asking for the moon. He remembered his father saying once, "It's what you expect from life you get, son," and he thought: Perhaps I'd better expect it. Sandstorm felt nervous. She eyed the ring suspiciously. However hard he tried, he couldn't imagine her jumping a clear round.

He wished now that he had jumped her first.

"That's one of Major Seely's horses, isn't it?" asked a man on a large ugly black.

"Yes. Sandstorm."

He didn't want to talk to anyone. He had always felt like that before going into the ring; it was as though he needed silence in which to collect all his energy and concentration, so that he could empty his brain of everything but the task ahead.

He tried to relax, but his sense of calmness had fled, to be replaced instead by a pit in his stomach, by a nagging doubt of his own ability.

But when his number was called again his calmness came back. He entered the ring as he had before, and again only the jumps counted. Somehow his calmness seemed to enter Sandstorm, who jumped the first three fences like an old hand. After the fourth jump each moment became an agony of suspense to David. Could she clear them all? It seemed too much to ask; and yet the dun mare didn't hesitate, but judged fence after fence perfectly, while David sat still, letting himself go with her strides.

He knew by a burst of clapping that he had done a second clear round. His first thought was: I wish Mum was here, because the moment would have meant so much to her – more, perhaps, than to anyone else.

45

He dismounted, stood shading his eyes with one hand, praising Sandstorm. Afterwards he would look back on the next few minutes as some of the happiest in his life, but at the moment it was a sense of relief he felt more than anything. Once again he had proved something to himself: he knew now that he was fit to ride Major Seely's horses; that show jumping was really his *métier*; that he was right in believing he belonged to the world of riding.

"Well done. That was really superb," said Major Seely.

"Congratulations. I've never seen her go so well. She was transformed!" cried Mrs. Seely.

He came back to reality. "She was wonderful. I just sat there," he said.

"There have only been four clear rounds, so you're in the running on both horses," said Major Seely. "I can only say: do the same again."

"In capital letters," added Mrs. Seeley.

He felt in a dream as he handed Sheila Sandstorm, mounted Tornado. He couldn't believe that he was here in Devon, changing horses after jumping two clear rounds. Success had always come to him as an appalling surprise, probably because he had never been much good at school – until he took up riding, almost the dunce of a clever family.

"I suppose one day you'll get over your inferiority complex," Pat had said once, "and discover that you can really ride."

But so far he never had.

He entered the ring again. The jumps were higher. Tornado knocked the stile, otherwise she jumped a clear round. He changed on to Sandstorm. A band was playing now. People were opening picnic baskets.

"Good luck," said Sheila.

Sandstorm was inclined to rush this time; several

A moment later he was back riding Sandstorm.

times she shortened her stride at the wrong moment; once she put her nose in the air and, taking command, jumped the triple at full speed. But because she was clever she always adjusted herself at the last moment and when she left the ring it was with another clear round to her credit.

He dismounted, but a moment later was called back for a jump off. This time there were only three fences and Sandstorm cleared them one after another.

He came out of the ring, thinking this is my day, one of those days when nothing can go wrong.

A moment later he was back riding Sandstorm, leading Tornado, being presented with first and third rosettes, his mind soaring into the future, imagining other rings, bigger shows, foreign stadiums.

When the congratulations were over and Major Seely had insisted that he and Sheila celebrated with a drink, he sat on the trailer ramp in a daze and ate the sandwiches Olive had made for him.

He felt quite limp, and too tired to listen to Sheila, who was talking as much as usual, now that Major and Mrs. Seely were having lunch in the refreshment tent.

In the trailer the horses munched feeds. David had taken off his coat, pulled down his braces and rolled up his sleeves. Later he would collect Tornado's prize, which Major Seely insisted should be his. He knew from the programme that she had won £5. He felt like putting it in the Post Office in her name, but was afraid that people would laugh at him. He had been brought up to save money against "a rainy day."

"It never hurts to have something put by, however little," his mother had often told him.

Even so, sitting now on the trailer, more than anything he wanted to buy a dog.

He suddenly wanted possessions: a dog, a bicycle – who knows, perhaps later a car.

"Here comes the governor. We'd better pack up. I don't believe you've been listening at all," complained Sheila.

He stood up and a wave of happiness came over him. The impossible had happened. He had won! Anything could happen now. Even his dreams might come true.

He thought of the letter he would write home, of how pleased the Bates would be, and his life seemed full of hope and opportunity, like the beginning of a perfect day.

The Second Show

The day after the show was rather an anticlimax. Tornado and Sandstorm rested. David schooled Jolly Roger and was told to take the afternoon off, and wandered along the lanes, suddenly lonely and homesick for Oxfordshire.

Three days later there was another show. This one was further afield and there was more bustle about the preparations. Mr. Booth plaited both the horses. David rose at five. This time Tornado boxed without trouble. Mr. Booth came instead of Sheila, and drove the car, because Major Seely was to come later, after visiting his office and answering the morning mail.

David travelled with the horses, preferring their company to Mr. Booth's, which seemed always to hold an undercurrent of hostility. The day was wet. Mr. Booth instructed him endlessly and kept him running

49

around for things like a stable boy. The course was tricky; David was wet to the skin before he entered the ring. All the same, both horses jumped a clear round and were finally placed second and third, this time Tornado above Sandstorm. It seemed to David then that his name was already half made. He could hear the experts talking about him, other competitors looking at him with envy, one rider saying, "Who's the boy Major Seely's found? He's someone to be reckoned with." He belonged now completely. The name of David Smith was on everyone's lips. In spite of the rain, and the fact that Major Seely hadn't arrived in time to see his performance, David was happy. Looking at Tornado, he kept thinking again: She's mine. And now he imagined riding her himself in foreign competitions, himself competing on his own horse, and it seemed that he could ask for no more, that once he had done that he would be at last content.

Travelling home through the wet afternoon, he thought of all the things Major Seely had said, and now there was a shaft of anxiety in the back of his mind, because next month Major Seely was going for a holiday in France, leaving Mr. Booth in charge.

"You'll go on just the same as usual. We'll work out a schooling chart for the horses before I leave; and you might go to a show or two. Then when I get back we'll start on the really big ones – the Royal, the Three Counties. You may have to sleep in the box. You won't mind that, will you?" Major Seely had asked.

The future had seemed like Paradise to David, until he imagined himself being organised by Mr. Booth. He wanted to say something to Major Seely, but what could he say? That he didn't like Mr. Booth? That Mr. Booth didn't like him? His anxiety hung over him like a cloud all the way home. He had a ghastly sense of foreboding. Now he realised that everything was working too perfectly, that life wasn't like that. He started to dread next month.

Sheila shrieked her congratulations. As they took off Sandstorm's bandages, he asked, "Did you know Major Seely was going away next month?"

"Yes. It's doctor's orders, apparently. He's been doing too much again. You know he's got a weak heart."

He hadn't known.

"That's why he doesn't ride any more," Sheila said.

"He doesn't look like someone with a heart," David said.

"Don't you like the thought of him going?"

"Not much." She understood, which made David's fears seem all the more real to him, though if anyone had asked, "What do you think's going to happen?" he couldn't have said.

"Well, don't let it get you down. Jimmy and I are behind you," she said.

He said good night to Tornado, walked to the bungalow with his hands in his pockets trying to rid himself of anxiety. But he couldn't forget how he had felt about Pat, how he had known weeks before she had said anything what was in her mind. And he had been right. He could only pray that this time his premonition would be proved wrong.

The next week-end he went home. The journey took four hours. He read *Horse and Hound*, and as he reached Oxfordshire felt as though he had been away for months instead of a few weeks. The trees were no longer in blossom; a few farmers had started to cut their hay. When he had left Oxford and was travelling in the familiar 'bus past fields which held so many memories for him, he felt really home.

51

He could think now: This is where I fell off. This is where Tornado bucked. This is where we quarrelled. This is where I took the pupils. It made him feel very old.

His mother was waiting at the 'bus-stop.

"Had a good journey? You look well," she said.

Everything was the same.

"Okay. Plenty of room. I had to change at Reading," he replied.

Tea was waiting on the kitchen table.

"Is Mrs. Bates looking after you properly?" asked his mother.

She went through his clothes, found a button missing, a seam which needed stitching. It seemed funny to sit there after tea watching his mother, to have no horse looking for him over a loose-box door, to have nothing to do.

"You're doing all right, then?"

He handed her *Horse and Hound*. Inside there was a photograph of him jumping Sandstorm. They were described as *a promising combination*.

"I always knew you'd do all right," said his mother.

He wanted to tell her about Mr. Booth, because he was still anxious about the future. But he didn't know where to begin.

"Tornado's won £20," he said instead.

"Well done. But don't you go spending it. Put it aside for a rainy day. You never know what may happen," his mother said.

He sat on in the kitchen, and started to think: What shall I do tomorrow? He wasn't accustomed to leisure. The week-end started to look very long. He wanted to say, "Heard anything of Pat?" But his mother didn't like her now, and, anyway, he was afraid to ask, because she might be abroad by now, or already engaged.

52

Presently his father came in, and there was a new pot of tea and they all sat round the table talking.

"Well, you've done very well, David. I can't say more, can I?" asked his father.

They were proud of him. He had given himself a reputation which he must live up to.

"Heard anything from Pat?" asked his father presently.

"No."

"I don't think she's here much now. Spends most of her time in London," his father said.

He saw Harringay, himself competing, Pat appearing from the stands to congratulate him. But that sort of thing only happens in books or films, he thought.

The next day was fine. He had no close friends in the village besides Pat, so he spent the day helping his father in the garden. In the evening he walked across the Common and remembered how he had schooled Tornado up and down the bunkers of the old golf-course.

He felt quite lost without a horse to ride. He had no other interests. He sat down on a bunker and thought about Tornado and watched the few rabbits scuttling among the gorse bushes.

On Sunday he put on his tidy clothes and went to church, which was something he hadn't done for years.

By this time he was glad to be going back to Devon. He wanted to see Tornado, to school Jolly Roger, to hear when he would be jumping again. He found he couldn't live without excitement now. He whistled as he hurried back to Sunday lunch, because by nightfall he would be back in Devon.

There was beef, three vegetables, Yorkshire pudding, fruit and custard. It was very hot in the kitchen. They sat with the door open.

"Now don't be late," said his mother. She had done

53

his packing. He kissed her on the forehead when he left, nodded to his father.

His mother had packed him a carrier full of food.

"Just a few biscuits, and an apple or two, and your favourite sweets," she had said.

He caught the 'bus, watched Oxfordshire slip past the windows. The train was late; he changed at Reading again. I wonder who's been exercising Tornado, he thought. I hope Olive leaves something out for me.

Mr. Booth met him at the station.

"Got back all right, then?" he asked.

David was the only passenger to get off the train. The air felt very soft, and in the distance he could see the purple hills of Exmoor.

"Yes. It's easy," he said. "Just change at Reading once you're on the express."

Tornado whinnied when he stepped out of the car.

"We turned her out to exercise herself," said Mr. Booth.

The Bates were out, but there was a cold supper waiting for him on the kitchen table. He sat down, thinking: It's not so bad to be back. Home's all right if there's something to do. . . .

"Can I come in?" called Sheila.

"Of course."

"I was wondering whether you still want a dog, because I've heard of one. The sheep-dog at the farm's got six puppies. Mr. Sellars says you can have the pick," she said.

"Sit down and have a cup of tea," said David.

"Of course, you may not want a sheep-dog," began Sheila.

"But I do," he said.

Presently they both went down to the farm, and he chose a puppy with a splodge of black over one eye and paid Mr. Sellars £2.

54

"I should leave it for another week. She's a bit small yet," said Mr. Sellars.

Walking back to the stables with Sheila, he felt very happy.

"How have things been going? Do you know when the next show is?" he asked.

"Mr. Booth was on about you. Said you didn't clean the tack properly. There's a show on Wednesday and the Seelys leave for the Continent on Saturday," Sheila told him.

"Then we're all at the mercy of Mr. Booth. Why doesn't he tell me if he doesn't like the way I clean the tack?"

"Because you're neither fish nor flesh. You're not really under him at all, because you're a pupil, not an employee," explained Sheila.

He couldn't see what difference it made, but quite suddenly he felt cold.

"He simply doesn't like me," he said.

For a moment the future looked bleak. He knew he couldn't stand a great deal of disapproval; it destroyed the confidence he possessed in himself, which wasn't much.

Then he shrugged his shoulders. There's not much he can do really. Major Seely's completely satisfied with my riding. He won't be away long, he decided.

"I must rush or I shall be locked out. See you tomorrow," called Sheila, disappearing into the dusk.

I wonder what I'm entered for on Wednesday, thought David. I really can't hope to do so well a third time. What shall I call the puppy? Thinking about his puppy, he went into the bungalow, cleared away the supper things and washed up.

Then lying back in a chair, he turned on the wireless and imagined himself riding with a sheep-dog at his heels.

The next show was a large one. There were agricultural exhibits, a huge variety of animals, vegetables, fruit, flowers – even a shoeing contest. There were two rings, and David was to jump in the main ring at three o'clock.

He felt nervous today, though he couldn't have said why. He had slept badly the night before and arrived late in the yard in the morning. Sheila and Mr. Booth had come. Major and Mrs. Seely were to follow later in their second car. Tornado was nervous too; she didn't like the smell of the other animals, the bleating of the sheep, the squeaks from a pen of piglets. Sheila led her round while David rode Sandstorm. It was another hot day, and the smell of the animals, the clank of machinery, the hot mass of humanity milling round the tents seemed to consume all the air until there wasn't any left.

They had left early in the trailer and travelled without a break until after one o'clock; now it was twenty to three and David couldn't rid himself of anxiety, couldn't stop thinking: Supposing we do badly today? Supposing I make a muck on both horses?

Major Seely arrived in plenty of time, and stood in the collecting ring with David, giving him advice. There was a thin corridor of space between them and the ring; the rest of the space round the ropes was packed six deep with people, except on one side, where the grandstand loomed large, filled to the brim.

The first prize was £50 and a cup. The entries were limited, but Major Seely had entered a long time ago, in the days when he still had Tony Booth.

"It's quite a simple course really; nothing tricky," said Major Seely, and David thought: People always think that if they're not competing. It's a different matter when you're about to meet the jumps one by one yourself. He had walked the course, one of the few riders without breeches and boots. He was to be the first competitor.

Nearly everyone seemed to know each other in the collecting ring, except himself. He felt conspicuous and a little lost – the first competitor, one of the youngest, the only one in sight in jodhpurs.

If I could win today with Tornado, I could get myself some boots, go to that place in London where Colonel Lewisham goes, have them made to measure in real calf, thought David, watching the spectators settling themselves more comfortably in the grandstand, the judges entering the ring, feeling suddenly sick, thinking: It's such a big show. Really, it's awful riding other people's horses.

"Well, best of luck, David," said Major Seely, going away to his car, while the Collecting Steward approached and they pulled back the rope which barred the entrance to the ring. He was ready now, all his energy concentrated on the effort he was about to make. His entrance was heralded by a fanfare. It was very hot in the ring; the grass looked parched. On all sides a sea of faces watched.

He cantered across the turf. People looked at their programmes; over all shone a sun from a sky flecked with the faintest, tiniest clouds. Sandstorm was eager. She took the first three fences a little fast, but faultlessly, like a well-balanced piece of mechanism. They cleared the oxer, the double railway gates, the triple bars;

David seemed to be toppling in a world of bricks.

David felt confident now and marvellously detached from everything but the job in hand. They approached the wall. They were half-way round the course. From somewhere in the crowd a little girl dropped a paper-bag, which fluttered across the ring. It was so small. Afterwards David could never decide what Sandstorm thought it was: A piglet? An enormous bloated insect? But now in the ring, she half stopped, dashed sideways, rushed on towards the wall, suddenly alarmingly close. She hit it full square in the centre, pecked, half recovered her balance and fell.

David seemed to be toppling in a world of bricks; then for a moment he was out, another second and he was in the midst of hoofs and tangled reins, thinking. What's happening? where am I? He was up before the stretcher arrived, saying, "No, thank you. I'm quite all right," calling everyone "sir" rather aggressively.

He looked round for his mother, before he remembered that he was in Devon, and, more dimly, leaving the yard in the morning. Presently he seemed to be sitting in the Seely's car drinking tea with sugar in it, about which he kept complaining. His head ached and the most important thing seemed to be the time and that he still had Tornado to ride.

He couldn't remember the time, not even when someone had just said "Four o'clock" or, "Nearly five." He couldn't remember whether it was Friday or Saturday, though it actually was Wednesday.

A doctor examined him, while he protested feebly, saying, "I'm all right. There's nothing wrong."

Presently he travelled home with the Seelys and was received by Olive, who seemed to be expecting him and hustled to bed, still asking the time.

He fell asleep at once and dreamed that he was jumping Tornado. When he wakened it was dark, but there was a plate of biscuits and a glass of milk by his bed. He couldn't remember very much. But he knew that he had met with catastrophe, and he guessed that he had concussed himself.

He was filled with gloom when he wakened in the morning. By the amount of light streaming through the curtains he knew that it was late. He tried to remember yesterday, but all he could recall was the bustle in the yard in the morning. The rest was a blank: only dimly did he recall travelling back with the Seelys.

Supposing I hurt one of the horses? he thought, climbing out of bed, pulling back the curtains, letting the sun into the room. He looked at himself in the mirror above the mantelpiece. He looked distraught, his hair was on end, but there was no mark on his face. He dressed and found Olive in the kitchen.

"So you've woken up at last," she said.

"What happened? Did I fall off?" Standing there, he had to know at once; the suspense was unbearable. Olive put down her duster. "Sandstorm fell with you," she said, and started to explain.

He didn't want to eat, but Olive had kept some breakfast for him in the oven – fried potatoes, sausage.

"You must eat something. Horses all fall sometimes. Surely you know that."

"Well, how are you feeling this morning?" called Jimmy when he entered the yard. "Proper silly you were last night."

Tornado was looking over her box door.

"How's Sandstorm?" he asked.

"Nothing wrong with her," said Jimmy.

He was teased all day.

"You certainly did go up the pole yesterday," said Sheila.

"Crackers by all accounts," agreed Jimmy.

"Never seen anything like it. The way you spoke to

60

the governor . . ." said Mr. Booth.

He wasn't allowed to ride. "You're to take it easy today, according to the governor," said Mr. Booth.

He went down to the farm and looked at his puppy, wrote to his mother. He still felt gloomy. It had to happen at the biggest show, he thought. Why couldn't it have happened to Tornado after I had jumped Sandstorm? He couldn't help thinking that his luck had changed. He hated having nothing to do. In the afternoon he helped Sheila clean the tack.

"Cheer up. It happens to the best people. Now, take Leonard . . ." she said.

On Friday, Major Seely worked out a schooling chart for the three horses with David.

"There's just one show I want you to go to while I'm away. Both horses are entered. If Sandstorm wins it'll upgrade her, and after that you'll be in the open classes," he said.

David had never ridden in an open jumping event. It would be another rung in his ladder to success.

"And don't worry about last Wednesday. It happens to the best of us at times," added Major Seely.

He walked round the horses with Mr. Booth, discussing their feeding problems.

Sheila and David stood together in the saddle-room.

"I wish he wasn't going. The moment he's gone, Mr. Booth will start throwing his weight about, you'll see," said Sheila.

"It's a horrible thought."

"The only thing is to have a sense of humour. Once you start fretting and fuming, you're finished," said Sheila.

The next morning the Seelys left at dawn. At first

there was a sense of relaxation hanging over the stables. No one hurried; David schooled the horses in a more leisurely manner than usual; Sheila found time to scribble a line to Leonard during the morning.

But by the afternoon Mr. Booth was running them all off their legs, most of all David.

"You may be a pupil, but you're a working one," he said once.

David didn't mind being corrected and harried in his stable work, but when next day Mr. Booth started to take an interest in Sandstorm's schooling, he began to feel uneasy.

"It's all worked out, Mr. Booth. The governor and I talked it over together before he left. Today I'm working her on the flat, tomorrow we're hacking, the next day schooling and jumping," he said.

"She's too fresh. You're not riding her enough. Take her out this afternoon. Let her have a pipe-opener," said Mr. Booth.

"I'm schooling Jolly Roger this afternoon," said David.

Mr. Booth watched him ride Jolly Roger. He seemed to have all the time in the world, now that Major Seely was away.

"You want to get him more collected. He's all over the place. He'd go better in a double bridle," said Mr. Booth.

"But the governor . . ." began David.

"That doesn't matter. I'm in charge now."

A cold shiver travelled swiftly down David's spine. He began to dread the next few weeks; they loomed ahead full of awful possibilities.

"And what I say goes," said Mr. Booth, leaving the school. The horses will be ruined quite quickly, thought David. I shall have to stand up to him. One must have a few principles. He was filled with a sense of futility. How will it end? he wondered.

Mr. Booth returned with a double bridle under his arm.

"But I have Major Seely's instructions," began David.

He thought: Everything's going wrong very quickly. First I concuss myself, then this happens.

"Are you in charge or am I?" asked Mr. Booth.

"I'm in charge of Jolly Roger's schooling." David rode Jolly Roger out of the school, down the drive, into the road without looking back, though he wanted to very badly indeed. He knew now that he had as good as declared war on Mr. Booth. It would be a fight between them now to the bitter end. He didn't expect to win; but one has to stick to one's principles whatever the cost, he told himself, and remembered his mother saying once, "If you do what's right, David, everything will come right in the end." He believed that now as he hacked Jolly Roger round the outside of a field. Somehow, everything would come right; Major Seely would understand. He remembered that he was to go to a show with Mr. Booth, that he had to work with him; the future looked complicated, and to forget it he sent Jolly Roger into a gallop, and switched his thoughts to cross-country events and imagined himself riding at Badminton.

He hacked slowly home. Mr. Booth wasn't to be seen, but Sheila seemed to be waiting for David.

"Whatever's happened? Mr. Booth's in an awful state. I thought he was going to throw a fit or something!" she cried.

"That's all right," said David, sliding to the ground. "He tried to make me ride Jolly Roger in a double bridle. I have my orders from the governor, and I'm sticking to them."

"Well, you've certainly put him in a mood. It's not much fun for the rest of us."

"One must have a few principles. I'm not employed by Mr. Booth," replied David.

"Have it your own way, but I wouldn't be in your shoes."

Jimmy wasn't encouraging either. "It's never good to quarrel with your superiors," he said.

"But David's only a pupil," said Olive.

"That don't cut any ice with Fred Booth," replied Jimmy.

"But Major Seely said . . ." began David.

"That don't make no difference neither. Fred Booth's in charge," said Jimmy.

It sounded very illogical.

"Anyway, the horse might go better in a double. Major Seely isn't always right," continued Jimmy.

"I see David's point of view," said Olive.

"You don't know nothing about it," replied Jimmy.

"I've had my orders from Major Seely, and I'm sticking to them," announced David.

"No need to get on your high horse," replied Jimmy.

David was suddenly sick of the subject. He was still certain he had done the right thing.

"Well, I shall stick to the chart, whatever anyone says," he said stubbornly.

"Okay. But you'll be heading for deep water," replied Jimmy.

"Don't frighten the boy," said Olive.

David stood up, put his cup and saucer on his plate. "I think I'll go for a walk now," he said. Outside it was still sunlit, and the air caressed his cheek as only Devon air does, and from the fields came the gentle baas of sheep.

He didn't feel like visiting the stables again. He felt as though he was slowly burning all his boats one by one. For the first time he thought: Supposing I lose my job? – tried to imagine himself returning home a failure. And it was too awful to contemplate. Better take a look at my puppy, he thought, turning towards the Sellars' farm, while in the bungalow Jimmy said, "He's heading for trouble all right, rubbing Booth up the wrong way."

The Last Show

The next few days were some of the worst in David's life. Mr. Booth ignored him completely; he seemed to be walking under a perpetual cloud. No one but Olive was sympathetic.

"You've brought it upon yourself," Sheila said when he complained. "If you'd had as many jobs as I have, you would have learned to take things as they come. After all, you could have told Major Seely when he came back what had happened."

"But Jolly Roger might have been spoilt by then," replied David.

"Not likely. Booth's schooled horses for Richmond."

"But Jolly Roger isn't a show horse."

Gradually things grew worse. Mr. Booth cut the horses' oats. Sandstorm's jumping deteriorated; David lost confidence in her and in himself. He tried to place her at her fences, which he had never done before, and she, muddled by a method she didn't understand, began to rush. Tornado with far less oats lost her speed and dash, which had stood her in such good stead in time competitions. She began to tip fences. This was the moment when David needed help and advice; someone to stand and call, "Leave her alone; sit still," to share the responsibility for the training

65

of two show jumpers and a promising One Day Event horse.

He thought of writing to Major Seely; he tried to remember everything he had ever read or been told about show jumping. He stopped jumping Sandstorm and Tornado for two days. Then Mr. Booth spoke to him.

"We'll be leaving at nine tomorrow. I'll do Sandstorm. You can look after your own mare," he said.

David replied "Yes, sir" without thinking, and immediately began to dread the morrow. He wanted to run after Mr. Booth, to cry "Need we go?" like a child who doesn't want to go to a party.

He didn't know the name of the show, where it was, how long they would have to travel. He felt quite lost, and each moment the future seemed to grow blacker.

"Well, aren't you pleased? Show tomorrow," called Jimmy.

"No. The horses are off their form," David shouted.

He thought: If only they were both mine; then nothing would drag me there. Why didn't I stay at home, take a job as a labourer and school Tornado in the evenings? At least I should have had some freedom then.

He thought: Probably Sheila's right, I was a fool to stand by my principles. If I hadn't quarrelled with Mr. Booth, he would have helped me school the horses, and if they were in bad form we needn't have gone.

He thought: When one comes down to brass tacks, it's generally one's own fault.

"Cheer up," said Olive when he went in to tea. "You look as though you'd just come back from a funeral."

"I feel like it," he answered.

He had no appetite for the potted meat-paste, the little fancy cakes, the large piece of yellow cheese, the sliced bread from the Co-op. He thought: I should have written to Major Seely. Why didn't I? I could have got his address from somewhere.

Olive poured him some tea. "Aren't you going to eat anything?" she asked.

He shook his head. He sat looking at the stained white tablecloth and saw his world of dreams toppling like a pile of bricks before his eyes.

He saw Sandstorm refusing three times in the ring; Tornado somersaulting over the wall. And everyone will say I lost my nerve the day I concussed myself, he thought.

"He's got cold feet about tomorrow," Jimmy told Olive.

"Can you tell me why Mr. Booth's been cutting the horses' oats?" he asked.

"Couldn't say," replied Jimmy, cutting himself a piece of cheese and reaching for the butter. "Why don't you ask him?"

Yes. Why haven't I? wondered David. Really, everything's my own fault. He stood up and, muttering, "I must clean my shoes," left the room.

"What's the matter with him?" asked Olive.

"Can't get on with Fred Booth. First of all he was cocky; now he's the opposite."

"I'm sorry for the kid," said Olive.

Much later he decided to visit Tornado. An awful feeling of loneliness hung over him, a black shadow separating him from friends and foes alike; his old sense of inferiority had come back. He felt empty inside, but couldn't bear the thought of food. Olive and Jimmy had gone to the local. He might have read a book to escape from reality if there had been one in the bungalow, but the only reading matter besides the *Daily Mirror* was Olive's magazines, which concerned themselves with romance and knitting patterns and occasionally babies.

He could hear Olive and Jimmy coming back as he walked to the stables. The night was clear. Another fine day tomorrow, he thought.

He crossed the yard, spoke quietly to Tornado, before he noticed that the light was on in the forage-room, though the door was shut.

"Back in a moment. I'll get you a handful of oats," he told Tornado.

He was about to open the forage-room door when he heard voices inside.

"I can't let you have another bag till next week," said Fred Booth.

"That's all right. The same price then – a quid?" asked his companion.

David stood frozen. "Yes. Okay by you?" asked Fred Booth.

"Okay. The chickens are laying fine on it."

David wanted to flee, but now the door was open, the light dazzling his eyes, Mr. Booth saying, "Hullo, who is it?" He couldn't speak. He realised a great deal now. He knew that he and Mr. Booth could never be anything but enemies for ever. He stood there feeling like an eavesdropper, and guilty, though he knew that right was on his side. He's a thief, he thought. He's selling Major Seely's oats. That's why the horses' rations have been cut. Do any of the others know? Sheila? Jimmy?

"So it's you. What are you doing roaming about at this time of night?" asked Mr. Booth.

David could move now. "Just taking a look at the horses. I saw the forage-room light was on," he answered.

"This is a friend of mine. I should get along to bed if I were you," said Mr. Booth.

He noticed a van parked by the yard entrance as he walked back to the bungalow. His mind was in a turmoil. He saw a hundred possibilities. Should he write at once to Major Seely? Send a telegram? He had no proof. Would Sheila support him if he told her?

He longed for Pat's company now. She would know at once what should be done. Perhaps he should write home for advice. The problem was still unresolved when he went to bed, not to sleep, but to lie tossing and turning till the small hours.

He wakened feeling like a limp rag. He got out of bed thinking: I wish there wasn't a show – longing more than anything to be able to go back to sleep. He didn't bother to comb his hair or wash his face, simply dressed and plunged out into the cool morning air in his oldest jodhpurs, a shirt, and braces.

Mr. Booth was already up. Jimmy and Sheila were starting to clean the loose-boxes. He was the last, unwashed, feeling too tired to care.

The events of last evening seemed far removed from reality in the morning light. Much more real and of greater importance was the approaching show.

David started to groom Tornado. "You'll have to do all the work today," he told her.

Because he felt untidy, Sheila appeared unusually spruce. She had curled her hair and her face was freshly made up.

"Feeling better?" she called to him across the yard.

"Okay. I'd like a chat later with you," he said.

He felt he had to tell someone what he had seen and overheard. Sheila wasn't reliable, but she must have an opinion one way or the other.

"Okay by me, if there's time," she said.

He was ready by nine o'clock. He found Mr. Booth already loading the horses when he appeared in the yard, his jumping hat and stick under his arm.

"Here you are, then," said Mr. Booth.

He travelled with the horses. No one had suggested that he should ride in the car, and he preferred their company. He knew now that they were competing in a reasonably large show sixty miles away. He had learned that much from Sheila before he left. He had had no opportunity to discuss his discovery of the evening before with her.

But when he left she had called, "See you tonight."

Travelling, he could only foresee disaster – refusals, fallen fences, himself falling off. Mr. Booth drove carefully and the journey seemed to drag on unbearably like a hideous, endless dream.

They were late when they reached the show-ground. David knew that as they entered the ground, by the loudspeaker calling his number, by the riders in the collecting ring, and by the competitor jumping the large, well-planned course. He found that he was sweating, that the dream had become a nightmare from which there would be no awakening except to the fact that it was reality.

"There's plenty of time," said Mr. Booth, getting out of the car.

But David knew there wasn't. His hands were shaking. He couldn't buckle Sandstorm's throat-lash; and the loudspeaker was still calling his name.

"Plenty of time," said Mr. Booth.

David wanted to scream "There isn't!" as he sprang into Sandstorm's saddle, cantered across to the collecting ring.

"You're late," said the steward. "Better go straight in."

His hands felt clammy on the reins. It was worse than a nightmare. Sandstorm was still stiff from the journey in the horse-box.

He rode straight in, saw the usual horde of faces,

70

women clutching bags, children sucking sweets, here and there a knowledgeable face mixed up with the crowd. Everything was the same, yet different, because for the first time he was afraid.

He turned towards the first fence, felt Sandstorm settle into her stride. He hadn't been able to study the course, he could only hope to follow the numbers. He let her choose her own pace, saying to himself over and over again, "David, don't interfere. Sit still. Leave her alone."

They cleared the first three fences before he lost his way. He realised too late that he was jumping No. 5 and heard the judge blowing his whistle with a sudden feeling of sickness.

"Will No. 46 leave the ring," announced the loud-speaker.

He felt like a whipped cur as he left the ring.

"Whatever happened to you?" asked Mr. Booth.

He couldn't answer, because he could only have screamed. "It's all your fault!" and he had been brought up to believe things were his fault, not other people's.

He mounted Tornado. Somewhere a band was playing Elgar's *Pomp and Circumstance*; in the ring a competitor was jumping a faultless round.

"Better do better this time," said Mr. Booth.

There was time to ride Tornado round the show-ground, to look at the other competitors, to remember that she was off colour, to pray for a clear round.

The feeling of sickness came back as he entered the ring. Tornado eyed the jumps without enthusiasm. There was a tightening in his throat, as though something was winding itself round his neck, slowly throttling him. He let Tornado go as she liked; she tipped the second fence, the third, the fourth.

He didn't care – didn't care about anything any

71

more. No one clapped as he left the ring; he was the last competitor; the loudspeaker was calling numbers for the jump-off.

"Well I never," said Mr. Booth.

David thought he caught a gleam of satisfaction in his eye. He dismounted on to legs which felt as shaky as stilts. Now we can go home, he thought. It's over. The worst has happened.

They boxed the horses in silence.

"No point in staying," said Mr. Booth.

What will happen now? thought David. I'll lose my job, I suppose. But it's not as bad as losing your legs, going blind, becoming mad. Lots of people live without realising their ambitions. He felt calm now, rather as though he had just emerged from fighting a rough sea – exhausted, glad only that he had survived. He thought: There are other jobs. Major Seely must give me a reference of some sort. He can say I'm honest, that I have enthusiasm – at least that.

He remembered the incident of the night before, and for a second it seemed that he held Mr. Booth helpless like a fly in the palm of his hand. Then he thought: But supposing no one believes me? I haven't any proof. Why should anyone believe my word against his?

They were travelling again now – much faster this time, it seemed to David.

I suppose Mr. Booth will write to the Seelys, he thought next. Probably he does regularly. Had we been friends, he might have found excuses. As it is, he'll write the worst he can.

They passed the moors, and lonely cottages standing by themselves like lost people who have pitched their tents in exposed places, unable to go on any longer. They passed through a town. The horses stood calmly munching hay. David remembered suddenly that he

72

hadn't eaten. He couldn't remember breakfast, and he hadn't eaten the night before. Probably Olive had put out a large package of sandwiches, but he hadn't seen them. He remembered his puppy. What could he do with her if he lost his job? What with Tornado?

I can go home, he thought.

Presently he saw the drive. The yard with its clock tower, the grey pigeons. They turned in. We're back, he thought, and braced himself to meet Sheila and Jimmy, while in one of the loose-boxes a horse neighed.

"I'm Back"

"Don't be so gloomy," said Sheila later as she and David stood together in the saddle-room cleaning tack. "You make the governor into such an ogre. He'll just think you need some more instruction. After all, he's show-jumped himself. He knows what it's like."

"If only I knew what Mr. Booth was going to write," sighed David.

He felt very tired. He wanted to sleep and sleep. He had found Olive's sandwiches and eaten them. Jimmy had handed him a letter from his mother.

"Write soon," she said. "People are always asking after you."

But he knew he wouldn't write until he had good news. Or until the news was so bad it couldn't be worse.

"Anyway, if you do lose your job you can always get another one," said Sheila with the voice of experience.

"But what about Tornado and my puppy?"

"They're a handicap, it's true. I suppose at a pinch you could sell Tornado."

73

But he knew he couldn't. It would be like selling a part of himself. She was tied up with his successful past, and he couldn't let that go. Looking at her, reminding himself that she was his, he could remember that once he had been a success, and what he had achieved once he might achieve again.

"Well, I'm knocking off. It's been a long day. Only three weeks now and then Leonard will be back," said Sheila.

She combed her flaxen hair, shrugged her shoulders.

"Well, good night, David. Don't always look on the black side."

He felt worse when she had gone. The awfulness of the day came rushing back and he had to remind himself again: It would be worse to lose my legs, to go mad, to be blind.

Tea was waiting in the bungalow.

"So you didn't do so well today," said Olive. "Never mind. You can't always win, you know. You mustn't be a bad loser."

She doesn't understand, he thought. She doesn't know how badly I rode. If only it was simply a matter of being a good or bad loser – if that was all.

"Better luck next time. That's what I always say," continued Olive.

It was a relief to find that Jimmy was out. He could let his mind wander crazily like a sleep-walker through the last month while she talked.

"What about the washing-up?" he asked when they had finished tea.

"It'll keep."

"I'm going to bed, then."

"What about supper?"

"Don't bother about me. I've had lots of tea, thanks all the same."

It was wonderful to climb into bed; to pull the bed-clothes up to his eyes, to feel like a wounded animal returning to its lair, a long journey over, to feel oblivion, to sleep and sleep.

Nothing happened for nearly a week. David rode the horses. His despair ebbed away. Perhaps Mr. Booth hadn't written, he thought.

He had told Sheila about Mr. Booth selling the oats.

"Gosh! Lots of grooms do that. If you'd seen some of the things some stud grooms do when the boss is away! Why, at one place the head groom was letting out the horses for seven-and-six an hour," she said.

"But didn't you do anything?"

"What could I do?"

"Well, write to the boss," said David.

"But I hadn't his address. Besides, what's the point of stirring up trouble? He was a jolly good stud groom, all the same," Sheila replied.

Sandstorm and Tornado were back on their proper rations. Mr. Booth spoke now to David, though not more than to give orders or to comment on the weather.

Then on a sunlit day when flaming June was living up to her name, and a cuckoo had been calling "Cuckoo, cuck, cuckoo" since early morning, and David had fetched his puppy and decided to call it Tina, his world collapsed.

Mr. Booth found him in the saddle-room.

"I've had a letter from the boss," he said. "He's not pleased by the way you're riding the horses. He can't come back for a month, and so he thinks it's better if you leave. I have a week's wages for you here."

For a moment everything seemed black. Is this really happening? thought David.

He couldn't think of anything to say – could only stand, seeing the future all too clearly, repeating to himself again and again: He thinks it's better that you leave.

"Of course, we're all sorry. That goes without saying," said Mr. Booth.

He wanted to shout, "You know that's not true. You've always disliked me because of your son, and later because I knew about the oats." But instead he muttered, "Thank you for telling me," as though it was a moment for politeness!

He thought: I've got the sack – and felt the shame which it had brought to his forebears to have to say the same thing. He took the money offered by Mr. Booth without noticing. The future held nothing but disgrace.

Presently David noticed that Mr. Booth had left. He had been fetching Jolly Roger's tack; he had planned a long ride; there seemed no point in riding now. He found he still had an egg-butt snaffle bridle slung over his arm. He hung it up, stood looking round the saddle-room, thinking: I've lost my job. What do I do next? Where do I go from here?

He wandered aimlessly round the yard, before he walked the half-mile to the nearest kiosk and found himself saying, "Is that the station? I want to box a horse to Oxford tomorrow. Is that possible?"

It took a long time, but when everything was fixed for seven-thirty in the morning, it was still only three o'clock.

"So you're leaving," said Olive when he went in to tea.

"That's right. Seven-thirty in the morning." He couldn't help feeling ashamed. None of his family had ever lost a job before. It was a matter of pride; it was possible to leave of your own free will, but to be given the sack was something which didn't happen to the Smiths.

"I'm ever so sorry. Never mind. Don't be miserable," said Olive.

She helped him pack. "Are you taking your horse?"

"Yes; and the puppy."

"Got anywhere to keep the horse."

"Not yet."

"I can't understand Major Seely. It's not like him. I don't trust Mr. Booth myself. Jimmy says he's all right, but . . ."

But what? thought David. "Mum's always said if you do what's right everything comes right, but I can't see it. Now now, anyway," said David suddenly.

"Well, there's still time," answered Olive. "I wish I'd known before that you were leaving. I'd have ironed some of your things. They look a proper sight, really they do."

The morning was grey, as grey and dismal as David's mood as he put his tack on Tornado.

Mr. Booth had offered to take the puppy and David's suitcase to the station in the car, an offer David could gladly refuse, since he had ordered a taxi for the purpose.

Olive had handed him a parcel of sandwiches and a thermos of tea.

"Don't bother to send back the thermos; we've got another," she said.

Jimmy and Sheila had said good-bye as a sort of

greeting when they arrived. Now he had only to leave.

He mounted, looked at the yard, rode out into the greyness of the morning. Tonight I shall be home, he thought. If there's nowhere else for Tornado, I shall have to ask permission to put her in the Hunt stables. He saw himself arriving at the cottage, his mother looking up from her cooking, crying out with surprise. Tomorrow I can buy *Horse and Hound* and start looking for another job, he decided. He came to the station, and there was the taxi with Tina looking out of the back window wriggling her behind. It was sleepy as country stations are in the early morning. Nothing seemed to stir; over everything hung the greyness of the morning which was soon to clear giving place to a perfect day.

He tried to forget that he was going home. Tornado could smell the smoke of trains and advanced in leaps and bounds. A porter emerged from a door marked *Parcel Office*. "Your truck's ready for loading," he said.

Presently he was sitting in the groom's compartment with Tina on his knee licking his face. Tornado watched him with large eyes. His suitcase lay beside him on the seat.

He wished now that he had written home. There would be so much explaining to do, and he didn't feel like explaining. He wanted simply to make another start.

He could see his father beginning, "Well, son . . ." His mother upset, but behind him with her bottomless faith in his ability to ride as well as anyone in England.

It was a long time before the horse-box left the station. When it did it was on the end of a long train, and swayed and jolted, while outside the sun-dried hay lying in cut fields and gilded hurrying rivers gold, and lit the countryside with brilliance, giving beauty to everything it touched.

David sat, going back over his past; remembering past failures, past mistakes, past catastrophe. He had no confidence in himself now, and there was no Pat Lewisham to cheer him, because she was in London or at Henley or Wimbledon being a debutante. He half-envied her now; to have no need to work for anyone, to be able simply to enjoy yourself, seemed to him at that moment the most important thing in life. A paradise which he would never reach, because he had very little money and no talent.

It was a long journey, or, rather, it seemed so to David. Tina shared his sandwiches, but he had nothing for Tornado except crusts of bread, and could sense her growing hungry as the hours passed.

As they drew into Oxford Station past the cemetery and the gasworks, he began to panic. Supposing no one will have Tornado? Supposing I drop Tina on the way home and she cracks her skull? he thought frantically.

But when he was out of the town riding with Tina perched in front of him on the saddle, he felt calmer. He remembered the popular song, *What will be, will be*, and at that moment believed it. It was evening now; the hottest part of the day had passed. Farm implements rested in fields he knew, had hunted across, loved. Cows grazed, no longer besieged by flies. In farmyards motherly hens took their chicks to bed.

I'm going home, thought David, and saw the cottage soft in the evening light, his room the same as always, the Common framing a sunset of red and burnished gold.

It was a long ride; Tina fell asleep quite soon and lay across his knees, her lips drawn apart, showing small baby teeth. Tornado smelt the countryside, walked easily with a swing to her stride, as though she knew that she was going home.

Tina fell asleep quite soon.

They passed the Hall, the drive to the Hunt stables, where Tornado hesitated; they came to the Common and saw the sunset, and that the gorse was still in bloom.

They rode down Church Lane, saw the cottage, Mr. Smith digging the garden, the back door open, smelt the flowers in the front border.

The church clock chimed the hour; among the graves an old man sharpened his scythe.

"Hullo. I'm back," called David, thinking: What will they say? Will they mind? Where shall I put Tornado?

Home Again

"It's David!" cried his mother, leaving the hot iron she was using on a snow-white pillow case, so that presently a smell of scorching arose and she had to flee indoors again. "Whatever's happened now? And you've brought Tornado too. Not that I'm not pleased to see you. Don't think that."

His father put down his fork, dusted his hands carefully on the seat of his trousers. "Been in a scrape?" he asked.

David dismounted. "This is Tina," he announced, holding out his still-asleep puppy for both of them to see. He felt the weight of the whole world hanging round his shoulders. It was one of those moments which would be with him for always, one of the worst in his life.

He couldn't look his parents in the face. He stood in the road shuffling his feet, a small boy again caught in the middle of a forbidden escapade.

"It's a long story," he said at last. "Do you think

Mr. Jackson down at the farm would put up Tornado for the night?"

"You haven't done nothing terrible? Stolen or anything?" asked his mother with a tremble in her voice.

David was hurt by the suggestion. He thought: She should know me better than that.

"Of course not. What do you take me for?" he asked.

"I don't know what I'm saying," she cried.

"It's worth trying Jackson," said Mr. Smith.

David kissed Tina, buried his face in the tiny ruff of fur round her neck.

"I've lost my job. That's all," he said. "It's a long story." Tornado stood eating the Smiths' neatly trimmed thorn hedge. The smell of half-dried grass drifted gently towards them from the churchyard.

"Well, I'm sure it wasn't your fault," said his mother, rushing indoors to save her pillow-case.

Presently David was down at Mr. Jackson's farm, holding Tornado, knocking on the back door, while Tina ate bread-and-milk in the Smiths' kitchen.

He had crossed the Common, ridden down the slopes where once he had schooled Tornado.

"Well, I'm willing to help you out for a day or two," said Mr. Jackson, and led David to an oblong paddock behind his house.

"She won't hurt the calves, will she?" he asked.

"No. She's never hurt anything," replied David.

He watched the bay mare roll. He didn't want to return to the cottage, to have to explain, to talk and talk, to listen to his parents' opinions, his mother's indignation; though in a way he was glad enough to be home.

He crossed the Common slowly, stood looking at the landscape, before he turned down Church Lane.

He found supper ready on the table.

"I expect you'd like to eat first and talk after," suggested his father.

His mother had found a cardboard box for Tina, in which she had put an old blanket folded four times. The puppy was asleep again, and David wished for a moment that he was Tina, well fed, asleep, with no worries and nothing to explain.

He ate the plate of fish his mother passed him with bread and butter. He drank three cups of tea.

"Well, this is how it happened . . ." he began, determined to tell his parents every detail.

The next day he caught a meandering country 'bus into Oxford and bought *Horse and Hound*. He still couldn't believe he had really lost his job. When he thought about it, his knees felt weak, and there would be a tight feeling in his throat and he'd think: But it's true, I have. I've had the sack – and the thought would make him stop in his tracks, so that once an old lady tripped over his feet in the High, and a little later he held up all the traffic in the Cornmarket.

On the way home he scanned the columns of *Horse and Hound*, marking two or three situations with a pencil.

It was another perfect day – too perfect for anxiety or sorrow. There wasn't a cloud in the sky, and Oxfordshire was a tranquil land of quiet, sunlit fields of cut hay, baled hay, hay being cut and baled and carried.

"Any luck?" asked his mother when he was home, slightly dazed from reading in the 'bus, from the crowds in Oxford, and from the journey which had revived so many old memories.

Sitting on the kitchen table he read out the advertisements he had scored with a pencil:

"Groom wanted for well-known show stable. Must be lightweight and able to school ponies. Good wage for right applicant. Wilts."

"That's not so far away. You could come home on your day off," said Mrs. Smith.

"Boy or girl wanted to assist in busy London riding school. Some experience essential,"

continued David.

"Groom wanted to help on farm in summer. Sole charge of point-to-pointers during winter months."

"They simply want a labourer. You would find you were doing the whole lot winter and summer," said Mrs. Smith. "Milking the cows and all."

"It's a bad time of year really," said David. "There's lots of jobs if only I could drive a horse-box. Otherwise most of them are for girls. If it was August I could get one in a Hunt stable tomorrow."

He sat looking out of the window, trying to imagine himself in London, schooling ponies in Wiltshire, hay-making.

"Isn't there another paper?" asked his mother.

"Not with the same sort of advertisements."

"Why don't you stay here a while? You know we like having you."

"I can't do that," replied David, jumping off the table. "There's Tina and Tornado to be considered too."

"Well, Tina's all right here . . ." began his mother.

"But Tornado isn't. Mr. Jackson only wants to have her a few days," cried David.

He climbed the stairs to his room, and in a mood of desperation replied to all three advertisements, stuffed them in his pocket and hurried to the post. He had written very little, simply stated his experience, mentioned Tornado and Tina, and said that he would only require pocket money and keep for his horse.

He felt a little happier when the letters had disappeared into the red letter-box at the end of Church Lane. But presently he met a friend of his mother's, who cried, "Well, David, it's good to see you. Your mother said you were home on holiday. How does it feel to be back?"

His first thought was: So Mum's ashamed of me losing my job – and he felt himself reddening and all the beauty seemed to have gone from the day.

"Okay," he muttered, hurrying away down Church Lane.

If I don't get any replies to my letters by Tuesday, I shall go to an agency, get anything, work in a builder's yard, on a farm, anywhere as long as I can keep Tornado and Tina, he decided.

During the afternoon he took Tina with him to see Tornado. The day seemed endless. Hours seemed to have passed since he was in Oxford, yet it was the same day, and there would be tomorrow and Monday – no chance of a reply to his letters till Tuesday. And then he would have to write to say, "Yes" or "No." He couldn't simply send a telegram saying, "Coming."

And by Tuesday Mr. Jackson might be tired of Tornado grazing in his paddock. And there would still be a great many tiresome arrangements to be made about trains . . . about an insurance card, because he had never had one, and there would be the long hack to Oxford Station again.

He felt very depressed, probably more depressed than ever before, though there had been plenty of bad moments in his life.

He remembered one of his brother's favourite quotations:

> Not by Eastern windows only
>   When daylight comes, comes in the light;
> In front the sun climbs slow, how slowly
>   But westward, look! the land is bright!

But it gave him no more hope now than his mother's "If you do what's right, David, everything will come right. You'll see."

That evening his father said, "Why don't you write to Major Seely yourself? Stand up for yourself. Tell him the truth."

"But I haven't his address," began David.

"It can be forwarded. He must have left an address. Stands to reason a busy man like Major Seely wouldn't go away leaving no address."

Why didn't I think of that before? wondered David.

"It seems like telling tales," David said.

"There's nothing wrong in telling the truth," replied his mother.

So he sat down and wrote:

"DEAR MAJOR SEELY, — I am very sorry indeed that I have lost my job, because I was very happy riding your horses and liked staying with the Bates. I am very sorry that I rode Sandstorm so badly at the last show. I think it may have been

86

because we were very late arriving, and the night before I saw Mr. Booth selling oats and was upset.

"Thank you for teaching me so much.

"Yours very sincerely,

"DAVID SMITH."

He took the letter straight to the post because he was afraid otherwise he might change his mind and throw it on the kitchen range.

When it was safe in the box he thought: I wonder what ructions that will cause, if any – and started immediately to think of things he might have said which all sounded much better than what he had said. But now, of course, it was too late to write another letter, so he walked back along Church Lane for the fourth time that day, thinking: I'll let Tina out. Then I'll go to bed. Thank goodness today's over.

Tuesday brought him a reply from the London riding school.

"DEAR MR. SMITH [the letter ran], – We were very pleased to hear from you. We have a spare box, so could take your bay mare, and your puppy could sleep with you or in the saddle-room.

"We have a stable of thirteen at present – four at livery, the rest our own – and you would be expected to escort rides as well as doing all the usual duties. We are shorthanded, so could you start some time this week, if you like the sound of the job? We suggest a starting wage of £1 and keep for the three of you.

"Yours very sincerely,

"MURIEL PAGE.

"PS. – If you could travel to Paddington, we would provide transport for the rest of the way.

"M. P."

David passed the letter to his mother and tried to imagine himself in London, and started to think about Pat and wonder whether he would meet her one day in one of the parks when he was escorting pupils.

"They sound in a great hurry. Are you going to take it?" asked his mother.

"Well, the others haven't answered, and Mr. Jackson wants Tornado gone by Wednesday," replied David.

"Couldn't you put her anywhere else?"

"But the others haven't answered. I can't wait till next week's *Horse and Hound*." He could see himself now in London, the bustle in the streets; he would be in one of the greatest capitals in the world; there must be compensations to be found for the loss of peace, fresh air, and dreaming villages.

"I can always leave if I don't like it."

"That's no way to talk," retorted his mother sharply. "I don't like to hear a son of mine talking that way. Get a bad name, you will. You're lucky to get a job as it is without a reference. When I was young, if you had no reference you were as good as finished."

He didn't listen, though. He could only think: I've got a job, anyway. For a second he forgot completely the thrill of the show ring, of the feeling that came over him waiting to go into the ring, that competing had always meant more to him than almost anything else.

Then it came to him with a rush, and, standing there, he thought: I'll never jump for England now. It's farewell show jumping. But I know now I'm not good enough. I probably never was. Devon was my testing-ground and I failed.

He sat down and wrote accepting the job at a weekly wage of £1. He looked up the trains, rang up the station from the kiosk and booked a box for Thursday. He added a postscript to his letter giving his time of arrival and posted it.

And then at last he felt free of anxiety. It's settled now. I can't go back on it, there's no sense in worrying any more, he thought, and with an effort shoved all his ambitions into the back of his mind, and thought: From now on I'm a groom in a London riding school, and that's good enough for me.

London

Thursday found David in a train again, determined to like his new job, "looking on the bright side," as his mother said.

Tornado had been difficult to box this time, imagining, no doubt, another long journey without food and water. But David had made plans in advance, and now she munched mixture hay from a hay-net, while Tina lay on the seat watching David. His mother had packed him plenty of food. Because he had only been to London once before, to the circus in the Pony Club 'bus, he was excited. He saw it as a city of pageantry, a place where anything could happen, but most of all as a city of opportunity.

There was no one to meet him at Paddington. The horse-box was shunted down a siding and left. The station was unbearably hot; people hurried by with cases, with umbrellas and newspapers under their arms. Trains were announced over the loudspeaker. To David it all seemed very far from Oxfordshire and Devon.

He longed for a drink of lemon squash, but didn't dare to leave the box for fear of missing Muriel Page. He fell to thinking about her. Was she young or old? Fat or thin? He imagined her slim, with neat, short hair, but when she came at last she was large, with her hair in a net.

"So you've arrived. You are David Smith? Good. The trailer's just outside the station. We'd better unbox your mare," she said.

She looked Tornado over. "Nice-looking mare," she said.

The trailer was a ramshackle affair, towed by an ancient Buick which had evidently known better days. The trailer ramp swayed under Tornado's hoofs.

"We don't use it a lot now. We used to when we went to shows, but we haven't time nowadays for gadding about," said Muriel Page.

David tried to smile; but there was a sinking feeling in his inside. Climbing into the Buick, he realised for the first time how hard it was going to be to say farewell to his ambitions.

"She'll be useful for some of our gentlemen," said Muriel Page, starting the engine.

For a second he couldn't think who she was speaking about; then he knew it was Tornado.

"You mean my mare. But she's difficult; she was vicious when I bought her. Didn't I mention her in my letter?" asked David. He knew he had: he had written very firmly, "She is only suitable for escorting rides."

"Oh well, we'll soon knock some sense into her," replied Muriel Page.

Tina looked out of the window at London. Thunder rumbled in the air. David felt stifled, too horrified by everything to speak. Gone was the golden city of opportunity. Instead, he saw Tornado becoming a

90

tired, overworked hireling before his eyes; himself no more than a groom working among listless, overworked horses.

Lightning flashed, thunder crashed; Tina tried to hide under the seat. In the streets people ran for cover as the first rain fell.

David decided to speak. "I'm thinking of your gentlemen's necks. The only time she was ridden by anyone besides myself, she bucked him straight off, and he was a well-known judge," he said.

"Oh well, we'll see. But in my experience work cures most things," replied Muriel Page.

David didn't speak again. The further they drove the drearier the streets seemed to become; then at last they turned into a mews and Muriel Page said, "Here we are."

Washing hung in one corner of the mews. David couldn't see any horses looking over loose-box doors; but there was a smell of horse and the sound of hoofs kicking against a wall.

"You've got a little room next to the harness-room," announced Muriel Page.

They stepped out of the Buick into the hot afternoon. David couldn't bear to think of Major Seely's stable-yard now, though he saw for a moment the large, clean loose-boxes, the shining heads and necks and remembered the air of spaciousness and comfort which seemed to hang over everything.

"We've got a stall ready for Tornado," said Muriel Page.

The stables were on all levels. There was electric light, peat bedding. The horses were not thin, but they looked as though they never had quite enough to eat. Tornado's stall was approached by a cobbled slope along which she walked gingerly, eyeing her surroundings with disdain. David's room was small, with a narrow bed covered by a dingy eiderdown. A wash-handstand stood in one corner, an old rickety chest-of-drawers in another.

"There's a gas-ring in the harness-room if you want to make yourself a cup of Nescafe or cocoa at any time. You have breakfast and lunch with us," said his employer.

He combed his hair in front of the cracked mirror above the wash-handstand, while Tina explored the room. He didn't want to think any more now. He could understand Sheila's attitude at this moment: a good job was worth everything in the world; he knew that now. He remembered someone saying to him once, "Never quarrel with your bread and butter," and he had quarrelled with his.

He called Tina. Muriel Page was saddling a big bony grey.

"Here. You must meet my husband. Sid, come and meet David," she called.

Sidney Page reminded David of a pointer dog; long and lean, with a nose which never missed a chance; he shook David by the hand. "I hope you like it here," he said.

The harness-room was full of dirty tack. The stalls needed cleaning. Tornado stood looking lost and bewildered. Her eyes seemed to reproach David when he looked at her, so that he turned away, hurrying to help his employers saddle horse after horse with dirty tack while outside the day seemed to grow hotter and fresh thunder rumbled louder even than the ceaseless roar of traffic.

At six o'clock clients started to arrive. First two girls straight from office stools. They changed in the harness-room into slacks and fashionable blouses. They were pushed on to the big grey, who stood patiently with drooping ears, and on to a roan cob which had pigeon toes and a mane which needed hogging. The horses left the yard reluctantly as a large car turned in.

"Here's Mr. Carruthers. One of our wealthiest clients," said Muriel Page.

Pupils continued arriving until eight o'clock, when at last the yard was empty except for David, Tornado and Tina.

David had his instructions: he was to clean the fourteen stalls, fill the water-buckets, put hay in the racks. Working, he lost all sense of time, though quite soon clients started to return, handing him their mounts, saying, "We'll be back the same time next week." Or "Are the Pages still out? Well, I'd better ring up." Or "You're new here."

A tall girl in jodhpurs walked round the stalls until she saw Tornado.

"Huh, a new horse by the look of it. A good-looker too. I'd like to try her next week," she said.

"She's mine. She's not for pupils, I'm afraid," replied David.

"But I'm not a pupil. I've ridden for years. You ask Mr. Page. I ride all the horses here," she replied.

David couldn't think of anything else to say. The day seemed suddenly unbearably long; the future stretched ahead of him, too awful to contemplate.

He began to clean another stall, and tried to remember when he had last eaten, and wondered why he had been stupid enough to take the first job offered him.

Presently the Pages came back with the beginners they had been escorting. David had finished the stalls; dusk had come, heavy with petrol fumes; the buckets were filled with water, the racks with hay.

No one suggested cleaning the tack. The horses were brushed over quickly with dandy brushes. The lights were switched off.

"I expect you're hungry. I'm afraid we can't offer you

a meal, because we're going out, but there's a very good fish bar just down the road," said Muriel Page. Her husband stood in the saddle-room drinking beer.

"Bit young to start swilling this stuff yet, aren't you, David?" he asked, showing a row of pointed decaying teeth.

David took Tina with him. The fish bar was crowded, but presently he was seated with a plate of fish and chips, a cup of tea, vinegar, bread and butter.

He sat eating looking at the other people, with Tina on his knee sharing his supper. And I imagined I might meet Pat, he remembered, and tried to laugh, but felt only a choking sensation in his throat and a piercing sense of loss which seemed to penetrate his whole being, leaving him without hope. Sitting there with Cockney voices calling to one another, while outside 'buses passed the window, and the street lights came on to compete with the fading summer sun, he thought: All these years I've been living in a kind of dream world, where people have helped me, found me horses, given me a start. I've never realised how lucky I've been, never appreciated the meal waiting for me every evening at home, never understood that the world was really quite different; that one must fight for everything in life. Sitting there, he felt that he was seeing life as it really was for the first time; he lost all sense of time watching the people come and go, until at last a woman in a white overall tapped him on the shoulder. "We are closing now," she said, pointing to the clock.

It was eleven-thirty. He plunged out into the street. People walked along the pavement arm in arm; shops were lighted. Two policemen passed and stopped further down the street to try a door.

David found his way back to his room, gave Tina a drink from a bucket, undressed, fell into bed. Somewhere below him a late Tube train rumbled, from the road came a screech of brakes. He slept, dreaming he was at home, at school again, being teased by the other boys for his love of horses, until suddenly the scene changed and two policemen pursued him through the streets of London waving truncheons.

The Meeting

The next afternoon David escorted two children on the only ponies at the Mews Stables, Cherry and Dicky.

Cherry was a chestnut mare of twelve-two and Dicky a little grey pony of just eleven hands. They were both quiet and elderly. David rode Tornado and took his pupils Timothy and Jean in the Park, around which ran a tan track provided for riders.

They were meek, well-washed children who had come accompanied by a nanny. Their riding clothes fitted perfectly and each carried an elegant riding stick. They answered politely when David spoke to them, but neither began a conversation on their own account. Tornado was strung up after nearly twenty-four hours in her stall; she was difficult to manage and started to buck the moment they reached the Park.

When she had settled a little David started to question the children.

"Do you know where the withers are?" he asked Jean.

She looked bewildered and answered in a whisper. "No. No, I don't."

Timothy had never heard of a throat lash, and neither knew that both their ponies were wearing snaffles.

In the evening the big grey was discovered to be lame.

"We'll have to change everyone round and use your mare. He'll do for Carruthers," Mr. Page said.

David put down the two water buckets he was carrying.

"She isn't reliable. Really she isn't." He knew he sounded unconvincing. He thought: What will Mum say if I lose another job? I can't go home again this time.

"Mr. Carruthers is quite a fair rider. He'll manage her all right," replied Sid Page.

There seemed nothing more to say. David picked up the water-buckets again, and presently with a dismal heart saddled Tornado with his own saddle. Further down in another stall the big grey, who had been given by someone the unsuitable name of Imp, stood resting a swollen foreleg.

Tina followed David like a shadow, small and tire-less, but with a worn look on her puppy face which made David feel guilty, because he knew now that London was no place for a sheep-dog puppy, that she didn't belong to the noisy mews and dusty streets, but to hills and wild valleys and windswept moors. He picked her up and stood stroking her until Muriel Page appeared and said, "Seven more sets of tack to go on yet, David."

He saddled more horses. He tried not to think about Tornado, to forget about the prizes she had won, but quite suddenly he thought, I'd much better sell her. Perhaps Major Seely would be interested if I advertised her in *Horse and Hound*.

"Which animal did you say I was to ride tonight?" asked Mr. Carruthers, walking through the stables.

"Lead her out, David," said Muriel Page.

He put down Tina, who was in his arms again. He

felt very small suddenly looking at Mr. Carruthers, who was tall, and looked taller because he was smoking with a long cigarette-holder. He wanted to say something and was overwhelmed by a desire to cry, "You can't ride her! She's mine!" But he felt suddenly like a small boy again, and forced back the words rising to his lips, and led out Tornado without a word.

"Quite a good sort. Where did you pick her up, Mrs. Page?" asked Mr. Carruthers.

Muriel Page answered in almost a whisper, so that David knew at once that she was telling a lie, most likely pretending she's theirs, he thought with a rush of bitterness.

"She's not an easy ride," he told Mr. Carruthers, pulling down the stirrups.

"Don't worry about that," replied Mr. Carruthers confidently. "I've ridden a good many." He mounted while David held the offside stirrup, felt in his pocket, handed David a shilling. "Odd sort of saddle you've put on her," he said.

"It's a jumping one," replied David.

"Would you like it changed? We can easily change it, sir," said Sid Page, coming forward all bows and obsequious smiles because Mr. Carruthers was the stable's richest and most regular customer.

"No. Don't worry, Sid," said Mr. Carruthers, kicking Tornado, riding out of the yard, while David thought: Perhaps she'll behave all right – and didn't know whether to be glad or sorry, because if she was good he was afraid she'd take more customers, more and more until she was just a tired hireling like the other horses.

"You see, David. All she needs is a little work," said Muriel Page.

David was suddenly too sad to speak. He picked up

97

"Odd sort of saddle you've put on her," he said.

Tina; stared at the stables, but saw only rows of jumps, himself on Tornado; the One Day Event, the last few shows he had ridden in.

"If you keep on picking up that dog, she'll give up walking altogether soon," said Sid Page.

Three hours later the Pages and David stood in the mews yard together. Every horse was home except Tornado.

David's face was devoid of all colour. He looked like a ghost; he felt too tired to talk, too tired for anything. He could only think: Something's happened to Tornado. Imagine her galloping through London traffic riderless, see her slipping, falling, hear the screech of brakes.

"It's not the first time Mr. Carruthers has stayed out late. If he likes a horse, he's inclined to go on and on, look up his friends, get a drink from a pub. Isn't he, Muriel?" asked Sid Page, going to the harness-room to pour himself a glass of beer.

"I'm going to look for them," said David, walking straight out of the mews, ignoring what Muriel Page called after him.

He ran to the Park, stood scanning the riding track without much hope. Why didn't I stop Mr. Carruthers riding her? Why haven't I more spunk? What's happened to me? he thought, hurrying across the Park to the West Gate, standing staring at the constant flow of traffic passing outside, suddenly deciding: I'll hand in my notice. I'm not going to stay with the Pages any longer. I've still got some of Tornado's prize-money left. I'll manage somehow. Nothing could be worse than life as it is at present.

He looked so odd standing in the gateway staring

at the traffic, that a woman asked, "Are you all right, dear? Not ill or anything?"

"I've lost a horse," said David.

The woman looked at him as though he was mad and hurried on.

David ran into the street. The shops were closed. Workers hurried home. Outside a cinema there was a queue. David felt a little mad. His life, his whole world, seemed quite shattered. Supposing I never find her. Supposing she's already dead? he thought.

I've been too proud, he thought. I was afraid to stay at home for fear of people learning the truth. I needn't have quarrelled with Mr. Booth. At that moment he nearly walked under a 'bus.

"Why don't you look where you're going?" the driver shouted.

"It's boys like you what cause the accidents," called a woman.

He was lost in a world which wasn't his. He didn't know where to go next, who to ask, "Have you seen a loose horse, please?"

He started to run, dodging people on the pavement, knocking over a bicycle which leaned against a kerb. Sweat was pouring down his face now. He was wearing his old clothes; he was beginning to look like someone on the run, someone hunted.

He stopped to ask a woman selling newspapers, "Have you seen a loose horse, please? Or a tall man riding a bay mare?"

"A horse, dearie? No I'm afraid I haven't. Thank you, sir," she added as someone pressed threepence into her hand and took a paper. "I should ask the police, dearie. They'll know if there's been an accident."

He glanced at her pile of papers to make
100

sure there wasn't a paragraph headed: *Well-known business man Killed in riding accident*. But though a baby had been murdered, a woman strangled and a Countess divorced, there was no mention of an accident.

"I should. Really, I should," added the news-vendor.

David said, "Thank you."

"There's a police station on the corner three streets down. Thank you, madam. Good evening, sir."

He left her still selling papers. He stopped to wipe his face with a handkerchief. Why didn't I think of going to the police before? he wondered. When I get back to the mews I'm going to hurl Pat's bronze horse away, he decided a moment later. It's brought me nothing but bad luck. And I'll never believe my mother's saying about if you do what's right everything will come right, not ever again, he swore to himself, looking frantically for a police station.

I must have missed it, he thought a moment later, entering a residential area, where large houses stood in gardens and the street was lined with trees. I'll look a fool if Mr. Carruthers turned up at the stables half an hour ago looking as cool as the Thames in winter, he thought.

A pram stood chained to basement railings. Two people in evening dress passed in a taxi.

"But it is," cried a voice. "I thought it was. Hullo, David. Whatever are you doing here?"

There were feet running towards him from behind. He didn't want to turn round; he was so afraid of being disappointed.

It can't be Pat, he thought. It can't.

"Whatever are you doing? I thought you were in Devon," cried Pat, halting beside him, out of breath from running, looking not a day older, just the same as always except for the clothes she was wearing, which were elegant compared to the patched jeans she so often wore in the old days.

"I've lost Tornado," replied David, and felt suddenly like breaking down altogether.

"Why are you here? Are you competing at the White City or something?" asked Pat.

"It'll take too long to explain now. I must find Tornado. Do you know where there's a police station?" David answered.

"No. But we can easily dial 999. Look. There's a kiosk just down the street," cried Pat, and started to run ahead of him, crying back over her shoulder, "We won't need any money if we dial 999."

They reached the kiosk. "You'd better do it," said Pat.

David dialled 999. "Fire, Police, Ambulance?" asked a voice.

"Police," replied David, thinking suddenly: But supposing she isn't lost after all. I should have rung the stables first. But he was through now, explaining, saying, "I've lost a bay mare. Yes. I think there's been an accident."

Presently he was outside again talking to Pat. "It's awful supposing she isn't lost after all," he said.

"I think you had better tell me the whole story," suggested Pat.

Walking along the street towards the Park, he told her everything; and as he told her a great deal of his despair ebbed away.

She listened in silence until he had finished. Then she said, "I think you've had a perfectly awful time. I feel like ringing up Major Seely this very moment. I can't believe things like that really happen."

"And what have you been doing? Oughtn't you to be going somewhere? Weren't you on your way some-

102

where? I don't want to delay you," said David, who felt much calmer now.

"No. I'd been out to supper. That's all. I'm not much good at being a debutante really. I'm not pretty enough. I want to see your puppy. She sounds sweet," replied Pat.

"I'm afraid she'll get distemper. That's another thing," he said.

"Haven't you had her inoculated?"

"She isn't old enough."

"What did the police say?"

"They're going to make inquiries. They'll notify the stables if they discover anything," replied David.

"Poor Tornado. London can't be her cup of tea."

"It isn't. She's beginning to look like a captive animal. And her coat's dull. A few more weeks at the Mews Stables and you would hardly recognise her," David said. "But I'm going. I decided that about an hour ago. I'm not staying. It's too awful. I'm going to get another job," he added.

"A jumping job," cried Pat. "You can't take another dead-end job. You're going to jump for England. You know that."

His confidence was coming back. He was certain now that he could never say farewell to show jumping. He was determined now to make another beginning.

"How much farther is it to the stables?" asked Pat.

"Are you coming the whole way?"

"Of course."

He was ashamed to let her see his squalid room. He didn't want her to see how low he had fallen. He didn't want her to see Sid Page with his fingers stained with nicotine and his beery eyes; nor fat, bossy Muriel Page; nor the thirteen tired hirelings.

"Oughtn't you to be somewhere?" he asked again.

"I'm coming to see your puppy and to find out about Tornado. Don't forget she was once more or less half mine," replied Pat firmly, as though she could read David's thoughts.

They hurried across the Park, and to David life was suddenly worth living again, though he couldn't understand himself. How had he got into such a mess? Why had he stood calmly by while Mr. Carruthers had ridden away on Tornado? Why had he ever taken the job, for that matter?

"I've been mad, haven't I?" he asked Pat.

"You mean getting in such a mess? Yes. You have rather."

He had time to look at her now. She was wearing a checked summer dress, toeless sandals; her hair was casually done. She wasn't so different from the Pat who had run the Elm Tree Riding School as his partner.

"I've done silly things too. I suppose it's all part of growing up," she said.

"But I've been so feeble, sort of lukewarm," he said.

She didn't contradict him. They reached the other side of the Park. The roads were much quieter. The sky was streaked with red and gold. At that moment London looked beautiful – dreamy, mysterious, touched with gold, almost the capital David had imagined when he took the job at the Mews Stables.

They passed the fish bar where David had eaten on his first evening.

"I hope Tina's all right," said David, remembering how she had sat on his knee and shared his supper. "I left her in my room."

"It would be awful if she was lost too," Pat replied.

And now the awfulness of the whole day came back to him: the dreary ride in the afternoon round and round the Park, the endless stalls to be cleaned, the moment when the Pages had decided that Mr. Carruthers was to ride Tornado. How he had felt watching Tornado go out of the yard; the hours of waiting for her to come back, the realisation that something had happened, the moment when he had left the mews, ignoring the Pages, hating the whole world.

He could see the entrance to the mews. Children were playing outside, though it was dark and quite late. Somewhere music drifted from an open window.

"We're nearly there. I don't know what sort of reception I shall get. I left without a word," he said.

"I suppose they're paying you almost nothing. You always have needed someone nannying you. You're hopeless on your own," said Pat with a grin.

They were there now. He could see the lights were on in the Pages' little untidy flat above the stables, which always seemed to smell of stale tobacco smoke, gas and wet clothes.

"Be prepared for the worst," he told Pat.

"I am," she said.

If only Tornado's there already, he thought, turning into the mews. With Pat to back me up, it'll be easy enough to give in my notice. If only she's there.

"I'm Not Staying"

But she wasn't. Her stall stood dirty and empty. The harness-room was piled with dirty tack and smelt of beer; a dirty glass stood on the window-sill.

105

David let out Tina. "Oh, isn't she sweet?" cried Pat.

"I'm not going to show you my room; it's too awful," said David.

He felt exhausted again now. His exaltation at meeting Pat was wearing off. Reality stared him in his face.

"Was Mr. Carruthers the sort of man to steal a horse?" asked Pat.

"Gosh! No. Look. That's his car," replied David, pointing to the enormous Jaguar which stood parked in the mews.

"Well, I suggest we start on the hospitals. The London Clinic first."

"The hospitals?" cried David.

"Mr. Carruthers must be in one. And as he's rich, if he had any choice, he most likely chose the London Clinic. Where's the telephone?" replied Pat.

"What about the Pages?"

"I'm not going to bother about them," cried Pat.

"But what are you going to say?"

"I'm going to find out exactly what did happen."

The London Clinic said that they had admitted Mr. Carruthers, who was suffering from slight shock after a riding accident. He had left at nine o'clock. They knew only that he had been thrown by a dangerous horse. They refused to disclose his home address.

"Now we'll have to find his telephone number," said Pat, replacing the receiver and picking up one of the Pages' directories. "By the sound of him, I should say South Kensington."

David couldn't understand Pat's remarks. But he was happy to have her take charge.

"Here we are. I bet that's him. Do you happen to know his initials?" she asked a few seconds later.

"No. He called Mr. Page Sid, but he was very

much the gentleman – at least, the Pages seemed to think so."

"Well, I don't. If he had any manners at all, he would have rung up here from the London Clinic."

"But perhaps he did."

"Well, you said you waited three hours, didn't you?" asked Pat, dialling a number on the dial David couldn't understand at all, since it seemed to be composed mainly of letters.

"He's gone out – obviously night-clubbing. The maid says he's had a nasty accident. A nasty horse bucked him off in a Park somewhere or other. I expect he's night-clubbing by now," said Pat a few minutes later.

"Where do we go from here?" wondered David.

Pat started to walk round the saddle-room biting her nails. "I'm surprised the police haven't found her by now," she said presently.

David could hear footsteps outside.

"Is that you, David? Wherever have you been?" called Muriel Page.

"Looking for Tornado."

Muriel Page was in her dressing-gown.

"I can't understand what's happened to her," she said in an exasperated voice. "I shall never forgive you if she's thrown Mr. Carruthers."

"And we'll never forgive you for letting him ride her," cried Pat.

"Who's this girl?" cried Muriel Page.

"Miss Lewisham," replied David stiffly. Standing there, he suddenly discovered that he hated Muriel Page to an extent which shocked him. "As soon as I've found her I'm leaving," he announced, feeling suddenly strong enough to face anything.

"You have to give a week's notice."

"Well, I am not going to. I'm not staying another hour once I have my horse."

"You'll have no reference."

"I don't care."

The telephone rang. Pat picked up the receiver. "Yes, it is. Oh good. You've found her, then. The Brewery Stables. Where did you say? Yes. I know. I'm sorry to have given you so much trouble. Yes. Well, that's something. Thank you very much."

She put down the receiver. "The police have traced Tornado. She's in a brewery stable roughly seven miles from here. She seems to have crossed most of London. They want us to leave her there till morning," she said.

"Is she hurt?" cried David.

"They don't think so."

He stood there in a daze, anxiety ebbing away. He picked up Tina.

"Well, that's something. Now perhaps you'll change your mind about this nonsense about leaving," said Muriel Page.

David was too tired to argue. He felt now that he only wanted to sleep on a comfortable bed, but his bed wasn't comfortable. He hated his room. He had risen at six that morning; he had worked all day; now he only heard Pat talking through a mist.

"He certainly is. He's coming to spend the night at my aunt's. I'm ringing for a taxi now," she said.

After that there seemed to be an argument. And at some time Mr. Page appeared.

"He can't leave, can he?" cried Muriel Page. "I won't have it."

"A week's notice is the rule," agreed Sid Page.

"Go and pack, David. Would you like me to help?" asked Pat.

He took Tina with him, bundled his few belongings

108

into his suitcase. Pat was waiting outside the door. "What awful people they are. Come on. Here's the taxi."

A moment later they were travelling through an almost deserted London.

"Won't your aunt mind?" asked David.

"No. She's the best-natured person in the world. Nothing upsets Aunt Jill," Pat replied. "You can have the spare room. It's always ready for guests."

He wanted to thank Pat for everything. He tried to make up a little speech beginning, "But for you . . ." But words wouldn't come. Nothing made sense any more. For a moment he imagined himself home, then he fell sideways asleep. He was too tired to eat. Aunt Jill appeared through a mist in a dressing-gown.

Pat shepherded him up lushly carpeted stairs into a room with flowered chintz curtains. She put Tina in an armchair, placing a blanket on it first.

"I should fall into bed," she said.

"But I haven't washed."

"Do it in the morning."

The room made him think of rooms he had seen in films. He undressed, put on his pyjamas. Once in bed, he seemed to be floating on a cloud. He felt Tina jump on to his feet before he fell asleep.

The sun wakened him. The room bewildered him until he remembered. He lay then feeling like someone in a book, out of this world, staring at the elegant dressing-table, seeing for the first time that there was a green basin, feeling like a millionaire, a king, a film star.

Tina had gone. He imagined Pat walking her, London alive outside, Tornado champing in the brewery stables.

109

Ten minutes later he was walking downstairs. He could smell bacon cooking and realised suddenly that he was ravenous. He thought: What do I do now? I wish Pat would appear. I can't even remember what her aunt looks like.

He had put on his best riding clothes, looked out of the window of his room, and seen that in this part of London there was little traffic besides a horse and milk trolley, taxis, an occasional car.

He thought: What a lot I shall have to tell Mum when I get home. Perhaps she'll stop hating Pat now. Or will she be furious at me giving up my j b?

Pat came in with Tina as he reached the hall. "Hullo. You're just in time for breakfast. Tina was whining, so I took her out for a run. She *is* sweet."

Aunt Jill presided over the breakfast table. "You look better this morning," she told David.

"You were hardly *compos mentis* last night," said Pat.

"What dreadful people you've been working for," remarked Aunt Jill, pouring David an enormous cup of coffee.

He didn't want to be pitied, so he changed the subject.

"How do we get to Tornado?" he asked.

"On a 'bus. We've worked it all out," replied Pat.

He ate a great deal, though he felt like sticking halfway through the coffee, because until now he had always had tea for breakfast.

"How are you going to manage to get the horse home? I'm afraid I haven't got room for it here. Pat darling, I must fly if I'm going to call at Fortnum's on my way to that fashion show," said Aunt Jill.

David tried to work out a plan.

"You can do anything you like except stable your

110

horse in my house, David. Stay as long as you like," said Aunt Jill as she left.

"We'd better ring up the station and see what they can do about a train for Tornado," said Pat. "Then I'll ring up home and say she'll be in the park till further notice. Swallow's there, so she won't be alone."

"Will that be all right?"

"Why on earth not? Come on. Let's telephone."

They managed to arrange a horse-box for three o'clock that afternoon. Then David collected his suitcase and they set off for the brewery stable, taking it in turn to carry Tina.

"It's lucky I met you," said David.

"I've been hoping you'd write for ages. I thought you'd write to say 'Thank you' for the horse. I thought of calling on your parents once to ask how you were, but I know your mother doesn't like me," replied Pat, staring away down the street along which they were walking. "I wanted to know how you were doing; then I saw the piece about you and Sandstorm in *Horse and Hound*, and knew you were all right, that you were going to jump for England one day just as you always said. You can imagine the shock I got when I met you last night looking on the verge of suicide. I couldn't think what you were doing. Here's our 'bus stop," she added, stopping.

"I've been pretty stupid really. Somehow I didn't think you wanted to go on knowing me. You going to London and all," said David.

"That wasn't all me. My parents have wanted me to for ages. They were afraid I'd turn into a Muriel Page," replied Pat.

"But you couldn't. Nothing could make you look like her," cried David.

They climbed on a 'bus, clambered up the stairs.

"I love travelling right on the top," Pat said,

111

thinking: He's changed. I don't know how quite, but he has.

I still don't understand her, decided David, but then I never have.

"Until I met you I had really said farewell to show jumping. Now I know I never can," David told her. "I thought I was no good."

"Even after you'd seen that bit about you in *Horse and Hound*? Major Seely's the man I can't understand. Surely he must realise Mr. Booth's crooked," Pat answered.

They changed 'buses. The day was warming up. Tired shoppers turned homeward laden with baskets, shuffling aching feet.

"I never got to know him very well, you know. I wasn't there long enough," David said.

They sat in silence, each thinking about David's adventures, until Pat said, "Anyway, if you want a reference, Daddy will give you one. Surely you've always known that. For that matter, I bet he could find you a jolly good job if you asked him."

"I'll remember that."

"This is where we get off again," said Pat.

The stables were at the end of a dead-end street. Clean and airy, high-ceilinged and well-ventilated, they were a pleasant contrast to the Mews Stables. A little man in breeches and gaiters greeted them. "You've come for the little mare, then. We put her in the box at the end. She seemed a bit reckless. I'm afraid your saddle's in poor shape," he said.

My saddle! thought David. He had forgotten about it, never considered that it might be damaged beyond repair.

"The girth's broke on one side too," said the stable-man. Tornado looked very small in the old fashioned box obviously built for an enormous dray horse. She was turning round and round, churning up the straw. She whinnied when she saw David.

"I'll get her harness for you," the man said.

"She's been beautifully groomed," Pat said. "Have you any money? We must give the stables a pound. Look at all the hay she's got."

They mended the girth with string. The tree of the saddle was broken; the reins had lost their buckle; one saddle flap was torn.

"Poor David, your lovely saddle," said Pat.

They thanked the stable-man, gave him a pound and said, "For her keep and your trouble and everything."

David mounted, rode out of the yard feeling like a free man. Tornado was sound; she walked with pricked ears. He had met Pat again and they were friends. He was never going back to the Mews Stables; with Colonel Lewisham's help, he'd find another job; hope ran through him like water down a thirsty throat, giving him strength to begin again. Third time lucky, he told himself, beginning to whistle softly.

"Hi! Wait for me," cried Pat. "Remember I've got your suitcase as well as Tina, and I'm not on the 'bus yet."

He took the case. "If you hadn't put on a dress, you could have ridden," he told her.

"I've only got dresses in London. How was I to know I was going to meet you and Tornado yesterday?"

"I'm like a bad penny. I always turn up again. We're both bad pennies, aren't we, Tornado?" he asked his mare, leaning forward to stroke her neck.

Pat thought he looked like he always had again now. Last night he had seemed suddenly old, but now the furrows had gone from his forehead, his hair was falling forward as it always had, and he was laughing, smiling like he had in the days when they had started their riding school.

She thought of him riding home from Oxford and how quiet the landscape would be after London, and how untroubled.

She thought of the cottage kitchen, which always seemed to smell of pastry, and saw Mrs. Smith rushing out to greet him. She remembered all the good things Maudie had said about David when he had gone, and how her father's stud groom said, "The yard isn't the same place without David. He's a good lad, and that's no mistake."

"I don't like to ride while you walk," David said.

"Here's my 'bus. See you at Paddington," cried Pat, seizing the suitcase and dashing away down the road, thinking: Everyone likes David except awful people like the Pages, and even they didn't want him to leave.

A Letter

They met at Paddington. The horse-box was waiting down a siding.

"I seem to spend all my time putting poor Tornado on trains," David said.

"While I was waiting for you I rang up home. It's all right. You can put Tornado in the park, and Daddy says of course he'll write you a reference," Pat said.

"Thank you very much."

"So I shouldn't rush into a job. You've got your prize-money. Surely you can stay at home for a bit."

He didn't like to admit that he was bored at home after a few days, or that his parents liked to think all their children were working, that they would be worried if the neighbours started to talk, saying, "I wonder why David Smith's at home. Why, only a few days ago he was on holiday. Don't say he's lost his new job already."

David knew Pat had never lived in his world. Nobody bothered whether she was working or not. Nobody cared. She doesn't really know what life is like, he thought. She's never wondered how she's going to buy the next meal. He felt much older than her now, almost grown-up as he boxed Tornado.

She gave him Tina, his suitcase.

"Thank you for everything. I don't know how to thank you enough," he said.

"Don't then. It's nothing. I may come down next week-end; if I do, perhaps we can ride together," she answered.

He saw them riding together down lanes they had both known since childhood.

"Oh, good. It'll seem like old times," he said.

"Exactly," replied Pat.

They stood together saying nothing until an engine was hooked to the horse-box.

"Time to say good-bye. All the best," said David then.

"Yes. Regards to your parents. Let me kiss Tina good-bye," answered Pat.

She said good-bye to Tornado and Tina, pushed her chestnut hair back from her eyes.

"Well, look after yourself," she said.

He climbed into the groom's compartment. "Pity you aren't coming too. It'll be cooler at the Hall than up here," David said.

The box was moving now. Pat stood waving.

"Thanks again," shouted David.

"Don't mention it," cried Pat.

He watched her out of the window, still waving, standing quite alone on the siding now.

Then he started to think of arriving home. What would his mother say this time? Would his father be furious? I've lost two jobs in a very short time, he thought, and nobody else in the family has ever lost a job. I shall soon be the black sheep. He looked at his saddle again, at his broken reins, and the wave of elation on which he had ridden all morning became less buoyant.

He thought: Pat is such an optimist. She brushes aside the difficulties in life as though they don't count. His future looked very ugly to him now. He was beginning to dread his approaching appearance in his home village, and he started to wonder how he was to set about acquiring another job.

So while Pat rushed back to her aunt's to change before a lunch date, David sat glumly in the horse-box, watching his future grow blacker each moment before his eyes.

I ought to sell Tornado. I should never have bought Tina, he thought. They're both a handicap when it comes to jobs. If you're a girl it's different. You can help a little in the house, look after children, have pocket-money, and your horse is welcome. People expect girls to have horses, but not someone like me. Travelling swiftly between Slough and Maidenhead, he started to feel bitter.

One needs money to get on, the right background, he thought angrily. The dice have always been loaded against me. One can't pretend not to notice the fact for ever when it's staring you in the face all the time.

The train stopped at Reading. He got out, bought himself chocolate, potato crisps, a pork pie, which he shared with Tina. Pat's got people like her Aunt Jill behind her, he thought, and saw his mother's work-worn hands kneading pastry. It's different for her.

He had never thought like that before. His successful elder brothers despised people who blamed circumstances for failure in life. But sometimes his father would say, "Oh, well. It's different for them," alluding to someone like the Lewishams. Now he agreed wholeheartedly with his father, ignoring the fact that he had Tornado and his pony Folly to call his own, that he had started from scratch and yet been able to jump his own horse at some of the biggest shows in England.

When they reached Oxford, he thought again: Yes. The dice have always been loaded against me. All my life I have had to fight.

Riding once more through Oxford with Tina on his knees again he admitted defeat. He was too angry and miserable now to enjoy the sunshine, or the well-remembered fields they passed presently. The horrible reality that he was jobless stared him in the face, obscuring the sun, killing the beauty of tall trees against blue sky, making the whole landscape hideous to David, making him think for the second time in about two weeks: I'm returning home a failure.

He tried to imagine jobs he might take, but now he couldn't think anyone would wish to employ someone like himself, plus a dog and horse.

I shall have to sell Tornado, he decided, and it was a relief to have made the decision. But that will take time, he thought a moment later. I shall have to advertise her. People will want to ride her. And supposing she bucks them all off? Whichever way he turned, there seemed to be an obstacle facing him; and each moment Church Lane was drawing nearer and he would have to tell his parents what had happened, and hear the comments of his neighbours. He could imagine them saying things like, "Fancy you

117

back already, David" and "When are you going to get fixed up with another job? Why don't you try the Labour Exchange?" as the weeks passed and he was still at home.

And once Mum was proud of me, he remembered. How she used to boast! Now people will be able to have their own back.

Presently he turned down the drive to the Hall. Swallow grazed alone in the park. He took off his broken saddle, called to Swallow, let Tornado go, watched the surprise in her eyes, until she rolled, over and over, again and again as though to shake the dust and dirt of London from her bay coat for ever and ever.

He thought: Lucky Tornado, living in the present, never dreaming that she may be sold. He turned back along the drive, because suddenly there were tears blinding him and he was ashamed of them, because he was almost grown up. Something told him then that if he sold Tornado he would give up the struggle, fade into obscurity, whatever Pat might say.

He watched Tina running ahead, smelt the rhododendrons on each side of the gravelled drive, thought: Dad will have just got in. They'll be having tea.

He met no one as he walked home, and the nearer he drew to Church Lane the slower his steps became. The cornflowers were out in the garden. Today the back door was shut, but from the kitchen came the smell of fish cooking.

London seemed far away now. He could hardly believe that he had spent the morning with Pat. He picked up Tina. He could hear the wireless now blaring out music into the summer's evening.

They'll never understand what it was like at the Mews Stables, he thought. He walked up the path, opened the back door, said, "I'm back again."

118

They both jumped up; his mother upset her cup of tea.

"What have you done?" she cried.

"Where have you sprung from?" asked his father.

He kissed his mother's forehead, said, "I'm sorry. I couldn't stand it. You've never seen such a place, and they started to use Tornado for the pupils. . . ."

"Well, sit down and have some tea," his mother said. "I'll make a fresh pot."

"No. Don't bother."

"You'll be getting a bad name, David. Couldn't you stick it any longer? You mustn't put your horse before yourself," said Mr. Smith.

"Well, now I'm going to sell Tornado. I've made up my mind," David said, and felt like weeping as he sat down at the familiar table between his bewildered parents.

"Sell her? But she means more to you than anything, that horse," cried Mrs. Smith.

He remembered buying Tornado, breaking her in, her first show; he saw her bay head and large, kind eyes watching for him in the mornings, whinnying when she heard his footstep; he remembered hunting her, her speed, her scope in jumping. But I'm going to sell her, he decided. Life isn't like I thought. There's no room for Tornado in my life any more.

"Switch off that darned wireless, Mother," said his father.

"Are you short of cash, then?" he asked David.

"No. Not yet, anyway." David wanted to be alone now; he wanted to think things out, reshape his life.

"Your puppy's grown," said his mother.

"Well, eat something, David," said Mr. Smith.

He forced himself to eat. Outside the church bells pealed. "Bell-ringing practice," said his father.

He was home, but in a sense it wasn't home any more.

119

The air was sad with disappointment. At this moment his parents seemed almost like strangers. The same clock ticked on the mantelpiece; the same flowered curtains met the same brown window-sill; the same black kettle sang on the black range. The cottage was the same as it had always been as long as he could remember, but always before his parents had been behind him. Now he could sense their disapproval; they were ashamed of their youngest son.

Forcing fish down his throat, he thought: Why did I come home? There must be somewhere else I could have stayed. Where do people go who have no home? I could have pretended to my parents that I was still in London, invented a story.

"Well, what are you going to do now? Where's Tornado?" asked his father.

"In the park. I met Pat in London. She's been wonderful."

"What, Pat Lewisham?"

"Yes." He realised now how wonderful Pat had been. "She took me to stay with her aunt. She saw me on the train this morning," he said, and now the whole episode seemed like a dream, a fairy tale. Pat thinks life should be beautiful, he thought; soon she'll be my only friend, or, rather, the only person I can turn to for help, the only one who will understand.

"How did you meet? Did you look up Susan while you were in London?" asked his mother.

It never occurred to him to look up his sister, probably because they had nothing in common.

"You might have gone to her for help."

"But I didn't go to Pat. I met her in the street." How fantastic it all seems now, thought David.

"Don't bother the boy, Mother. He looks to me as though he needs a good night's rest. Everything will look different in the morning," said Mr. Smith.

"I'm sorry. I couldn't have stayed there even if the Pages hadn't put Mr. Carruthers on Tornado. Mum, you should have seen what I had for lunch and breakfast – cold pilchards, corned beef and old spuds. And I had to get my own supper. I never finished till ten o'clock at night, and was up at six each morning. I couldn't have stuck it," David said, seeing all the horrors of the Mews Stables before his eyes again – the endless stalls to be cleaned, the dejected horses, fat Muriel Page and her lean, shifty husband swilling beer. "Their place smelt like a pub does in the early morning," he added.

"Then you were right to come home. I wasn't happy about you going, was I, Dad? I can't help wondering what the neighbours will say, though – you back in less than a week and all," said his mother.

David had Tina on his knee now. He couldn't eat any more. He fed his puppy with bits from his plate.

"Let them talk. Some of them haven't so much to talk about anyway," said Mr. Smith.

In a sense, the worst was over now: he had told his parents. But he was still jobless. Dreadful days stretched ahead; tomorrow he must begin: advertise Tornado, perhaps advertise himself.

"Young professional rider seeks post. Experienced. Good worker. Excellent reference. David Smith, 10 Church Lane."

He needn't mention Tina till everything was almost settled – that is, if anyone answered his advertisement.

Tornado, he could say, was a promising jumper and One Day Event horse. He could list her winnings. People must have seen her. The trouble would start when prospective buyers desired a ride. But perhaps he could sell her over the telephone. He had heard of people buying horses like that without seeing them. But would that be honest? he wondered, seeing himself boxing Tornado once more, but now for the last time. He could feel tears rising behind his eyes; in a moment he would be crying; he stood up ashamed, clutched Tina, while an awful wave of despair engulfed him completely, leaving no room for anything else. Once he had believed that dreadful things didn't happen as long as you were honest, worked, told the truth. Now he didn't believe anything – least of all that if you did what was right everything came right in the end.

He felt his mother put her arm round his shoulder. "You're ill, David. That's what you are," she said.

But he knew he wasn't – not physically, anyway. He just felt as though there was nothing left of his dreams. "I'm all right, Mum."

The church bells had stopped ringing now. He thought of Tornado with Swallow in the park; like old times, he thought. If only we had never given up the riding school. I could have gone on alone. Why didn't I?

"What are you going to do next?" asked his father.

"Advertise myself and Tornado, I suppose."

"I've just remembered something," said his mother. "That letter for David. Where did we put it, Dad? We didn't have your address. You never left it."

A letter, thought David. Nobody ever writes to me.

"It had a Devon postmark," said his mother, routing among the collection of vases, David's past trophies, and a mug saying *From Bexhill* which stood in a cluttered disorder on the mantelpiece.

It won't be good news, thought David. It can't be from Major Seely. Perhaps Sheila's invited me to her wedding. All the same, his heart had started pounding

122

with excitement and with the first gleaming rays of hope.

"It came just two days after you left. Perhaps I put it on the dresser," said Mrs. Smith.

David started to search too now – frantically, as though his life depended on the letter.

Tina, imagining a game was afoot, began to rush round the kitchen yapping joyfully.

"Did you take it upstairs, do you think, Mother? Maybe you put it in his room," said Mr. Smith.

David ran upstairs with Tina yapping at his heels. Then he heard his mother call:

"David, I've found it."

I mustn't hope, he thought. It's sure to be bad news. He ran downstairs, took the letter, looked at the postmark.

"I think it's from Major Seely," he said.

His hands were trembling. He tore the envelope open and read:

"DEAR DAVID, – I was shattered to receive your letter. But first let me apologise for not having written to you before. Unfortunately, I was rather ill on first arriving in France and I could make neither head nor tail of Mr. Booth's letters. My wife and I were very surprised, however, when we received one from him saying you had left of your own free will.

"As you may guess, we came to the conclusion that you didn't like being at Hampton House and that there was nothing we could do about it.

"But, to cut a long story short, now we're home and, with the co-operation of Jimmy and Sheila and Olive, have got to the bottom of things. Mr. Booth has gone, and if by any chance you're free and can forgive me for the shocking way you've

He tore the envelope open and read—.

been treated, would you consider returning at increased pocket money of £2 a week and, of course, with your puppy and Tornado?

"Hoping you'll say yes, I've entered Jolly Roger for a One Day Event and I've been jumping Sandstorm on the lunge and she is in great form.

"Kindest regards from us both,
    "Yours very sincerely,
        "RICHARD JOHN SEELY."

"Look," cried David. "Look," handing the letter to his parents, thinking: Everything's all right. I needn't sell Tornado. I'm not a failure after all. I can go on show jumping, One Day Eventing. . . . I can begin again.

"It's just as I always say. If you do what's right everything will come right in the end," said Mrs. Smith, handing back the letter with eyes full of tears.

"Well done, son," said his father, reading the letter slowly, reading it twice, three times, looking at David as though he was seeing him for the first time.

The Visitor

Next morning David rose early and, with Tina at his heels, ran to the nearest kiosk to put through a call to Devon.

Major Seely was fetched from his bath.

"I'm sorry to telephone you so early, sir," said David "But I only saw your letter last night."

"Are you coming back to us?"

"Yes. I'd like to very much."

A great many pleasantries followed.

"Well, come as soon as you can. I'll put a cheque

125

for your horsebox in the post this morning," said Major Seely as the pips sounded for the second time.

David walked back to the cottage seeing himself, as he had so many times before, riding for England. Nothing seemed too difficult for him now, nothing impossible.

The past few weeks were nothing to him now except a bad patch in his life which was over. When he met Mrs. Emmett, whom he had known as long as he could remember, he found it easy to smile and ask after her health and tell her that he was returning to Devon very soon.

He felt free – freer than he had for months. He thought: While I'm here I'll go over to Milton and have a look at Folly. How lucky I am to have a horse, a pony and a dog!

His mother had cooked an extra-special breakfast when he returned to the cottage, and the sad atmosphere of the evening before had gone, to be replaced by a feeling which David could only describe as similar to that which always hung over them at Christmas or on a birthday.

After breakfast, when he was upstairs combing his hair before he walked across the Common to the Hall, his mother called, "There's a visitor to see you, David."

And now he could hear Pat laughing in the kitchen.

He ran downstairs.

She was standing talking to his mother. "I've heard your good news. Isn't it wonderful? I came back last night. London was stifling," she said, turning to David.

She was dressed in riding clothes. To have her there was like putting the clock back six months.

"I thought we might go for a ride this morning. What do you think?"

126

A moment later they were walking across the Common together.

"I couldn't believe Major Seely had really given you the sack when you told me. Now you'll be all right," Pat said.

"What about you?"

"I shall stay a bit longer in London. Then I may take a job. I don't know really. I haven't decided," Pat said, starting to chew a blade of grass. "Perhaps I'll go abroad. We might meet at a horse show. Wouldn't that be fun? Supposing we met in Paris? I should feel so smart knowing you if you were jumping for England. I should feel very proud."

"Do you remember me schooling Tornado up and down here?" asked David.

"Yes. Doesn't it seem years ago?"

"Yes. Years."

They walked on together, and it seemed to David, that he had almost everything he could ask for in life, that in a matter of a few hours his life had somersaulted from disaster to success.

And I nearly gave up, he remembered, but, as Mum would say, everything has turned out for the best in the end.

"I shall come and see you some time in Devon. I've got friends near you I can stay with," said Pat.

"That'll be lovely," replied David, imagining Pat "nannying" him as she had in the old days, biting her nails and tearing her hair with excitement.

STRICTLY FOR PONY-LOVERS

Now you have finished this novel you know what an excellent story-teller Christine Pullein-Thompson is. She really makes her characters come alive! And the horses – well, they're almost like people (only nicer!)

Dragon Books have published seven of her novels. Three of them, *The First Rosette*, *The Second Mount* and *Three to Ride*, make up an exciting series dealing with the adventures and misadventures of David and Pat.

David's whole life is bound up with horses, and his one great ambition is to ride for England. Things go wrong, of course, and at times he even thinks of giving up his dreams and taking an ordinary job like anyone else. But Pat believes in him and he has other friends, besides his ever-loyal animal companions.

Can he achieve what he has dreamed of for so long? Will he wear the British colours? Read the stories and you'll find out!

The Empty Field is also about ponies, only here the real heroes are three beautiful shire horses, condemned to be shipped abroad for slaughter.

The pony-lovers from the local riding school form a gang, and the story tells how they endeavour to thwart the ruthless smugglers who want to steal the horses. There are thrills galore in this book, for all who love ponies and adventure.